It was time to wake up!

When Leah reached the trees, she plunged headlong into the concealing foliage. Still running, she dodged limbs and jumped over fallen logs. The sound of her pursuer crashing along behind her gave her all the incentive she needed to push herself beyond her normal limits.

Suddenly she tripped and fell painfully to her knees. Before she could struggle to her feet, rough hands grabbed her from behind, and then she was being dragged into a thick clump of flowering bushes. She dug her nails into the hands holding her and kicked at her attacker with her bare feet. She was preparing to scream when her assailant finally spoke.

"Stop that," a disturbingly familiar voice snapped. "And will you kindly take your claws out of me?"

Leah froze. After a moment she turned her head slowly. When she saw the man who held her, she could only murmur in disbelief, "Mr. Gregory?"

Dear Reader,

Sophisticated but sensitive, savvy yet unabashedly sentimental—that's today's woman, today's romance reader—you! And Silhouette Special Editions are written expressly to reward your quest for substantial, emotionally involving love stories.

So take a leisurely stroll under the cover's lavender arch into a garden of romantic delights. Pick and choose among titles if you must—we hope you'll soon equate all six Special Editions each month with consistently gratifying romantic reading.

Watch for sparkling new stories from your Silhouette favorites—Nora Roberts, Tracy Sinclair, Ginna Gray, Lindsay McKenna, Curtiss Ann Matlock, among others—along with some exciting newcomers to Silhouette, such as Karen Keast and Patricia Coughlin. Be on the lookout, too, for the new Silhouette Classics, a distinctive collection of bestselling Special Editions and Silhouette Intimate Moments now brought back to the stands—two each month—by popular demand.

On behalf of all the authors and editors of Special Editions,
Warmest wishes,

Leslie Kazanjian
Senior Editor

BILLIE GREEN
Time After Time

Silhouette Special Edition

Published by Silhouette Books New York

America's Publisher of Contemporary Romance

If, then, true lovers have been ever cross'd,
It stands as an edict in destiny
            —Shakespeare, *A Midsummer Night's Dream*

SILHOUETTE BOOKS
300 East 42nd St., New York, N.Y. 10017

Copyright © 1987 by Billie Green

ISBN: 0-373-09415-9

First Silhouette Books printing November 1987

America's Publisher of Contemporary Romance

Printed in the U.S.A.

BILLIE GREEN's

college professor once told her that she was a *natural* writer. But her readers and editors find it hard to believe that she writes one good story after another only because she comes by them naturally. Maybe someday this devoted wife, mother of three and romance writer *extraordinaire* will create a heroine who is a writer. Then, possibly, we will get a hint of her trials and tribulations.

Chapter One

The actors are at hand:

A Midsummer Night's Dream—Act V, Scene 1

What in hell is this supposed to be?''

Leah, who sat on the other side of the desk, looked up from the papers she had been examining and took in Mr. Gregory's frown. The notorious frown. The same one that drew the eye away from the hawklike nose and the unusual green eyes. The same one that warned Universal Air underlings to either run and hide or find a damn good explanation for whatever had displeased the vice president of marketing.

She rose to her feet in an unconsciously graceful movement and walked around the desk to stand beside him. The north Dallas skyline, seen through a wall of gold-tinted windows, framed her as she glanced over his shoulder at the paper he held.

"Sorry, that wasn't supposed to be in there," she said. "Posner was having a bad day—trouble with his girlfriend, I think."

"I don't care if Posner is having trouble with two dozen Egyptian belly dancers," Paul Gregory said flatly. "If he can't do better than this, he shouldn't be working here."

Leah turned her startled laughter into a discreet cough. If timid little Leonard Posner were ever confronted with twenty-four dancing girls, he would faint dead away.

Leaning forward, she picked up a sheet of paper from the file in front of him. "You mean like this?" she asked, outwardly calm. "I had Leonard do it again. It was my fault the original wasn't discarded."

The look in her superior's eyes assured her that he had never doubted for a minute that it was her fault. Shaking her blond hair back over her shoulder, she moved a step to the side. Being this close to him always made her uneasy; a little like standing on the edge of an active volcano.

She glanced down at her watch. "Do you need more time to look through these? There's an exec meeting in ten minutes, but I can skip it if you want me to stay."

"That won't be necessary," he said, closing the file. "I've seen enough."

That doesn't sound promising, Leah thought, keeping her expression bland. Rule number one—never show fear to a predator.

He handed her the file. "Except for that piece of trash from Posner, it looks as if this might work. I'll expect to see a cost analysis and revenue projection on my desk tomorrow," he added without even glancing up.

Leah didn't say that getting those two things together by tomorrow would keep her working half the night. She didn't say that "this might work" was not exactly overwhelming praise for a project she had been working on night and day for more than two months.

She didn't say those things because neither of them even entered her head. Leah had worked under Paul Gregory for more than four years. She knew that if her work on this report hadn't been A-number-one, topnotch material, she would not be walking out of his office now; she would be slinking out with her tail between her legs.

"Miss French?"

She was at the door with the file under her arm when he called her name. Pausing, she glanced back. "Yes, sir?"

"I see you're up for the associate VP job in San Francisco."

"That's right."

Leah's classical features showed none of the excitement and none of the anxiety she felt over the possible promotion. The move from airline advertising executive to associate vice president in charge of public relations would be a major step in her career, the kind of step she had been working toward for more than four years.

"You'll get it," he said casually. "There's no one as sharp in the running." He frowned, the subject forgotten as he went back to his work.

Seconds later, Leah stood in the outer office in a bright purple daze. Mr. Gregory had almost paid her a compliment. Did that mean he would give her a good reference? she wondered, biting her lip.

She had no way of finding out, because she was too proud to ask, and he certainly wouldn't volunteer the information. Knowing her boss, he had probably meant that the people up for the promotion were all idiots, but that she was the least idiotic of the bunch.

One floor below, in her own office, Leah took a minute to freshen her lipstick before going to meet with the other advertising executives. Her work area in no way compared with the understated luxury of Mr. Gregory's. It was merely a twelve-by-twelve-foot room with gray carpet, and without a single window. But Leah was sinfully proud of the room. It was a real office, not a cubicle. And outside the office was a secretary. The fact that she shared Charlotte with two other executives didn't matter. Nor did it matter that Charlotte was too fainthearted to put off unnecessary calls. All that mattered was that Leah had a secretary.

After blotting the pink lipstick, she gave a short, breathless laugh, shaking her head. She was still slightly unnerved by Mr. Gregory's parting comment. It had never occurred to her that he would give more than a passing thought to her promotion. In the time Leah had been with Universal Air, she and the VP had occasionally worked together on projects—not often, but often enough for her to have formed definite opinions concerning his character. Paul Gregory wasn't the kind of man to take notice of what his people were doing unless it directly affected the work they were doing for him. He had a reputation for being a man with a will of iron who didn't try to disguise his fiery wrath when he encountered the failings of mere mortals. His rigid personality had prompted the people who worked under him to label him—behind his back, of course—Vulcan, after the Romans' dark god. He possessed the heat of the forge and the cold, unbending strength of steel.

Although his sober-faced pronouncements were sometimes startlingly funny, by no stretch of the imagination did he intend them to be, and he would use his notorious frown to wither anyone who dared to laugh. As a result, Leah had quickly absolved him of having anything as human as a sense of humor.

So, according to Leah's estimation, Mr. Gregory had neither a sense of humor nor a high regard for his fellow man. What he had instead was one of the sharpest minds in the country, and for that Leah admired him wholeheartedly. She was as single-minded about her career as her boss. Although she would rip out her tongue before letting him know, she had used Paul Gregory as a role model since first coming to Universal Air.

Her brow creased in thought as she leaned back in the black vinyl chair. Deep down, Leah was afraid she would never really be like her iron-willed role model. She tended to bubble rather than growl, and as often as not, her frown trembled at the corners and stubbornly became a smile. And her sense of humor insisted on embarrassing her by popping up at the most inappropriate times. No matter how she tried, she simply couldn't project a cold, stern image.

A last quick glance in the mirror assured her that her image—good or bad—would hold up for a while longer. Grabbing her briefcase, she left her office for the meeting room down the hall.

The executive meeting didn't take as long as she had anticipated. Even after Leah had taken a few extra minutes to try a few ideas on her associates, she was left with enough time to leave the building for lunch—something that happened perhaps twice a month under normal circumstances. She usually asked Charlotte to have a sandwich sent up from the coffee shop in the lobby.

She had just walked into the busy Italian restaurant two blocks from the Universal building when she heard her name being called. Glancing around quickly, Leah spotted Tanya Brice and three other women from the office waving frantically at her from a table in the corner.

As soon as Leah reached them, she pulled a free chair from a nearby table, and the four women shifted to make room for her.

"Wait until you hear this," Tanya said, leaning forward eagerly. "Shelley says Lester brought a six-foot brunette into his office this morning and locked the door...and they were in there for *two* hours."

Leah rolled her eyes. She wasn't overly impressed by Lester Walker's amorous adventures. As far as Leah was concerned, he was an incompetent fool whose only function at Universal was to provide everyone else in the building with an unending flow of material for gossip.

"That's not all," Bitty said portentously. Her real name was Betty, but her lack of stature had provided a nickname she couldn't shake. "Guess who caught Shelley with her ear at the keyhole?"

Leah glanced at the tall redhead across the table. Shelley groaned, covering her face with her hands. "I thought I would pass out. It would have been a relief to pass out," she added, shuddering. "He gave me the Frown and I froze—I mean it, Leah. I absolutely froze."

Leah had no need to ask who had caught Shelley. Her laugh had a rich, throaty sound. "I love it. And wouldn't I have given my Aunt Nola's girdle to have been there to see it." Her golden-brown eyes sparkled as she imagined the scene. "What did you say when he caught you?"

"What *could* I say?" Shelley asked helplessly as she shoved back her short, curly hair. "Mr. Gregory leaves me tongue-tied at the best of times. There I was on my knees, with my ear to the door. I looked up and wished there were a history of heart attacks in my family so I would have a chance of dying on the spot.''

Leah paused to give her order to the waitress, then turned back to Shelley. "What did Mr. Gregory say?"

Shelley giggled. Her wholesome, attractive face was red from a mixture of laughter and embarrassment. "He said—you know, with that killer tone of his— 'When you're through praying, Miss Koznovski, I'd like to see Walker's report on the traffic at Orly Airport.' "

The whole table broke up. Paul Gregory would not be pleased to learn that he had provided them with so much amusement, Leah thought, then immediately changed her mind. The man probably wouldn't care one way or the other.

"Oh, my God!" Tanya gasped. "Speak of the devil—Lord, I hope he didn't hear us."

Glancing around, Leah saw her superior pass their table with an older man of medium build. The two men were ushered to a secluded booth that Leah knew was always held for Paul Gregory.

"I don't care what y'all say. I think he's the most gorgeous man I've ever seen. He always reminds me of Heathcliff."

The comment from the fourth woman at the table brought a fresh round of laughter. Faith Noble was nineteen and had been a typist at Universal for three months. The other members of the group made fun of Faith's wide-eyed innocence and would deny with their last breath that she brought out protective instincts in them, but they weren't fooling anybody.

As the others began teasing Faith, Leah took a minute to study her boss. Heathcliff? she thought, tilting her head as she stared at him. Dark brown hair...dark features...was there a hint of cruelty about his strong lips? Leah had never cared much for the sulking hero of *Wuthering Heights*, but she could see that there might be a resemblance.

At that moment he glanced up and met her gaze, frowning slightly. Leah quickly looked away. No, not Heathcliff, she decided, swallowing a nervous laugh. Mr. Gregory portraying a romantic hero in the grip of an all-consuming passion was more than even her imagination could take. Vulcan he was, and Vulcan he would remain.

As she shook out her napkin, her thoughts went back four years to the first time she had ever seen him. It had happened on her first day at Universal. At the time she had been only three years older than Faith, and to be perfectly honest, she supposed she had probably felt a little like the younger woman did now.

No, that wasn't honest enough, she scolded herself silently as the other women talked around her. Faith had a crush on Mr. Gregory. That came nowhere near what Leah had felt. She had taken one look at him, and it had been like being kicked in the stomach. It was scary and exciting all at the same time, bringing a flush to her face and a peculiar flutter to her chest.

She had found the sensation too overwhelming for comfort and had been almost relieved to find that he was married. She didn't—then or now—have time for emotional involvement and wasn't the type—then or now—to indulge in casual affairs. Pulling up a little iron will of her own, she had buried the attraction. By the time his wife had died in a skiing accident a little more than a year after they had met, their relationship was solidly professional.

"Stop laughing," Faith protested indignantly as they continued to tease her about her fantasies. "I think he just pretends to be cold because he's still grieving for his wife. Everyone says they had a perfect marriage. That they were made for each other." She sighed, her eyes dreamy. "I think it's so beautiful and so tragic."

Tanya raised an arched brow. "Honey, you've just waved a red flag in front of our blond bull here." She grinned at Leah. "Come on, Leah. Tell Rebecca of Sunnybrook Farm what you think of men and women being 'made for each other.'"

Leah leaned back in her chair, glancing around the table at the expectant looks of the four women. She smiled slowly. "I think it's a crock of—I think it's nonsense," she amended hastily for Faith's benefit. "There is no such thing as a perfect marriage. Mr. Gregory and his wife might have had a good marriage—I don't know enough about it to have an opinion—but they were not made for each other." She took a bite of pasta, her face thoughtful. "Larger-than-life love, love for all time, is a fairy tale that has caused more American relationships to fail than any other single thing you can name. If a husband or boyfriend is a no-show in bed, it's because he's not Mr. Right. If he doesn't make enough money or he drinks too much, he's obviously not that One Everlasting Love. When the relationship gets rocky, what does the woman do? Does she examine the problem, whatever it is, and work to help fix it? Not on your life. She dumps the poor sap and goes out looking for the other half of her soul," she finished with mild derision.

The older women had heard Leah's opinions on this and a dozen other subjects before, but they loved egging her on. She could use logic to debate any subject, taking any side she or the others wished. For the most part, it was merely a verbal game, a party trick. But this time, Leah wondered if she didn't half believe what she was saying.

"But how can you talk like that, Leah?" Faith asked, frowning. "Look at Romeo and Juliet—"

"That's fiction. It doesn't count." Leah waved the suggestion away with one slender hand.

"Okay," Shelley said, her face eager as she threw herself into the subject. "What about the Duke and Duchess of Windsor? Ha! I gotcha this time."

Leah shook her head, grinning. "First, ladies," she said, nodding to her audience, "consider the proposition that maybe he wasn't really keen on the idea of being king in the first place. In that case, abdicating would have been no great sacrifice. He couldn't very well say 'Gee, guys, I don't think I want to be king after all.' No, instead, he latches on to the first ineligible female to come along and claims her as his one true love."

She took a sip of Chianti, carefully formulating her thoughts. "That's only one of my theories, you understand. Let's say it happened just the way everyone believes it did—the man gave up a crown, plus a lot of power and worldly considerations for the woman he thought he loved more than those things. Once he had taken that step, then what? The whole world was watching, for heaven's sake. Think how embarrassing it would have been to admit that they got on each other's nerves, or that her personal habits made him retch," she finished, her eyes gleaming with impudence.

Everyone except Faith was laughing. She looked a little stunned. "No—no, it couldn't have been that way," she said, her plump face set in belligerent lines. "You don't know anything about it."

"Of course I don't," Leah agreed without hesitation. "But neither do you. I'm just saying it's a possibility. The fact that they stayed married isn't proof that they had the perfect love. They had no choice but to stay married."

"I don't believe you. And I'm glad I don't," Faith said softly. "The world would be a lonely place without love."

"Oh, Faith," Bitty said in exasperation. "Don't take it so seriously. This is just talk—like gossiping about Lester, only on a bigger scale."

"According to Les, nothing bigger exists," Tanya said dryly.

All five of them sputtered with startled laughter. Leah knew it was time to change the subject, but for some reason she couldn't let it go. She felt just as protective toward Faith as the others did, and didn't like the possibility of the younger woman getting hurt because of her unrealistic dreams.

"I didn't say love doesn't exist, Faith," Leah said, leaning forward. "I simply said love between a man and a woman lasts by sheer determination and sometimes by force of habit. There is no great plan. By all means, fall in love. But be realistic about it. Don't expect to find something that transcends time and space. Be happy with a man you can bear to face across your cereal bowl every morning."

Faith grinned, looking suddenly mischievous. "I'll take Mr. Gregory. I would love to wake up to him every morning."

The resulting hoots and groans caused the people at the surrounding tables to glance curiously in their direction.

"You innocent," Leah said, her brown eyes sparkling with humor. "The man would chew you up and spit you out, and there would be little bits of Faith all over Dallas."

"But I would have died happy," Faith said with a silly grin; then she paused, studying Leah. "I really can't believe you don't think he's attractive. You're working with him every day now. Hasn't he ever... well..."

"Put the make on me?" Leah suggested. "Patted me on the rear and said 'Hey, toots, how's about I jump your bones?'"

"No," Faith protested, laughing. "Hasn't he ever asked you out? You're beautiful and—well, classy." She glanced down at her own chubby figure. "And thin. If I looked like you, I'd go after him in a minute."

"And you'd fall flat on your face," Leah said, her voice dry. "I doubt if our adorable VP even knows I'm female. I'm a working machine. And if I don't do the work, I'm a dead machine."

She glanced down at her watch. "Oh, Lord," she groaned, standing abruptly. "I'm supposed to view the tapes of the new presentation in five minutes."

After fumbling in her purse, she threw a ten-dollar bill on the table. "I'll be your best friend if you'll pay for me—someone, anyone. Bless you, my children. Oh, God, I'll never make it. I expect change from that ten," she called over her shoulder as she hurried away.

She had almost reached the door when she collided solidly with Mr. Gregory. "Excuse me," she muttered breathlessly, giving the man with him a harassed smile as she rushed out the door and broke into a sprint.

By the time she reached the office building, the luncheon debate was forgotten, but Leah recalled it later and wondered if she had mortally offended the god of love with her impudent monologue. Some strong force was obviously at work, because the rest of the day was an unqualified disaster.

The proposed presentation was supposed to be shown at a conference that was only two weeks away and was of such substandard quality that even she, who was used to tackling incompetence, couldn't believe it. And as if that weren't enough, the files she needed to compile the figures for Mr. Gregory had disappeared into thin air, causing her and Charlotte to spend the rest of the day searching for them.

Leah had eventually discovered the missing papers under a girlie magazine on Les's desk. And on the floor. And behind the wastebasket. Instead of helping her, he had tried to explore new territory while she was on her hands and knees under his desk. The resulting explosion was probably heard in Houston and had left Lester pale and gratifyingly subdued.

It was after seven before Leah finally managed to find a stopping place in her work. Shadows were gathering in the corners of her office as she stuffed the files into her battered briefcase and slipped back into her shoes.

As she walked down the hall toward the elevator, the rest of the building was unnaturally silent, reminding her of a line she had heard years before. *The last living cell in a dead body.*

The thought made her laugh aloud, and the sound came back to her as a muffled echo. The emptiness didn't bother her. She loved the place, bustling or dead.

Since the doors were locked at six she had to call Mr. Timms, the night watchman, to unlock them for her.

"How many times this week does this make?" he scolded, shaking his head. "You and Mr. Gregory are neck and neck as to who can work the longest hours." He glanced behind her. "See what I mean?"

Looking over her shoulder, she saw her boss stepping from the elevator. She raised a hand in response to his stiff nod and left the building.

When she walked into her apartment thirty minutes later, she didn't stop to sit down. She merely tossed her briefcase on the coffee table as she passed it on her way to the bedroom. After carefully hanging up her green linen suit, she headed for the shower.

Later, when she reentered the living room, she wore a blue nightgown that barely reached her thighs, her feet were bare and her hair was pulled to the back of her head in a less-than-neat ponytail. She walked straight to the kitchen and began pulling things from the refrigerator for a salad.

On the nights when she brought home work from the office, her routine was always the same. She didn't have to think about it; every movement had become automatic.

Five minutes later, back in the living room, she placed the salad and a glass of cider on the coffee table and walked to the bookcase opposite it. Opening one door, she exposed a portable television and a VCR.

On a shelf below the television was a stack of videotapes. She took the top one and inserted it. After playing it, she would remove it and place it in a different stack. Then, when they were all played, she would start over again. She never even knew what movies she inserted. It didn't matter, because Leah never watched them. Although she never admitted it, even to herself, the movies kept the apartment from feeling quite so empty. The sound of a human voice, even in a movie, was comforting.

As she sat at the coffee table, glancing through the papers, she quickly ate her salad. Leah knew she ate too fast—it was a habit she shared with many busy, ambitious people—but there always seemed to be something more important that needed her attention.

In the next few hours she broke away only once, and that was to carry the dishes to the sink, rinse them and stack them in the dishwasher. The rest of the evening she spent bent over her work.

At five minutes after eleven she stood and stretched her back. It was done, she thought. Walking to the television, she wondered how long the screen had been filled with gray static. She pulled the tape from the machine and placed it in the empty space beside the others, then closed the cabinet.

Leah was satisfied with her day's work. In fact, she thought smugly, she was satisfied with her life. How many people could honestly say that?

Switching out the lights, she walked to the bedroom and pulled back the cover on her bed. She had trained her mind to work for her and could usually fall asleep at will. Tonight, however, she still felt wide-awake. The project wouldn't let go of her mind.

Stubbornly she closed her eyes and waited for sleep to come.

* * *

Seconds later, when she opened them again, Leah had to blink several times at the bright sunlight. She rose slowly to her feet, feeling the soft, springy grass beneath her toes.

"Wow!" she breathed in awe.

She had never fallen asleep so quickly. And whoever it was who said dreams reflected the tensions of the day obviously didn't know what he was talking about. She had had a hellish day, and this was one beautiful dream.

The area where she stood was open ground, but fifty yards to her right was the beginning of a thick, shadowy forest, and straight ahead, in the distance, were gently sloping hills. The air she breathed into her lungs was as fresh, crisp and intoxicating as new wine.

For several seconds she merely stood and stared. She had never had a dream in Technicolor and was stunned by the spectacular beauty surrounding her.

At that moment a crackling noise behind her caused her to spin around abruptly, almost losing her balance in her haste. Instantly a gasp caught in her throat, and her eyes widened in astonishment. There, not ten yards away from her, was a leather-clad, shield-toting, card-carrying Roman gladiator.

Leah's first impulse was to giggle. In one hand he carried a round shield, in the other a net. He wasn't much taller than she was, but he was built like an ox. Muscles bulged across his bare chest, shoulders and thighs.

But as she took in the expression on his face, amusement died swiftly. The visor of his metal headgear was raised, and his gaze was trained on her barely covered breasts. While she stood mutely, he examined the long legs that showed below the short gown, then returned his gaze to her breasts and took a step forward.

"Hold on a minute, mister," she said, then began to back away warily.

He simply grinned and took another step toward her. For an interminably long moment, Leah couldn't move. Events seemed to take place in slow motion. It was the strangest sensation. The gladiator continued smiling and walking, and Leah simply stood watching him.

She tried to say "Let's talk about this," or "Can't we reach some kind of compromise?" but it seemed her voice was suspended, as well.

Then, whatever had held her still, released her. Her breath left her in a whoosh of relief, and she whirled around and ran. She didn't even consider talking to him now that she could move. This was obviously not a man open to rational discussion, she told herself, heading toward the safety of the forest.

As she ran, she thought she heard the net hiss through the air and hit several inches behind her, but she wasn't about to turn around to check. When she reached the first of the trees, she plunged headlong into the concealing foliage behind it. Running instinctively, she dodged limbs and jumped over fallen logs. The sound of her pursuer crashing through the brush behind her gave her all the incentive she needed to push herself beyond her normal limits.

"Damn!" she muttered sharply when she tripped over an exposed root and fell painfully to her knees.

Before she could struggle to her feet, rough hands grasped her under the arms, and then she was being dragged into a thick clump of flowering bushes.

In panic, she dug her nails into the hands holding her, kicking back at her attacker with her bare feet. Sucking air into her lungs, she was preparing to scream bloody murder when her assailant finally spoke.

"Stop that," a disturbingly familiar voice snapped in her ear. "Ouch! You little fool, will you kindly take your claws out of my hands?"

Leah froze. After a moment, she turned her head slowly, a frown of confusion adding creases to her normally smooth brow. When she saw the man who still held her, she murmured in disbelief, "Mr. Gregory?"

Chapter Two

I have had a dream—past the wit of man
to say what dream it was.

A Midsummer Night's Dream—Act IV, Scene 1

Mr. Gregory,'' Leah stammered again; then her voice dropped to an astonished whisper. "Mr. Gregory, you're wearing your *pajamas*."

He stared at her for a moment in blank silence, then his eyes began to sparkle with amusement. "Only the bottoms," he said, chuckling softly. "I don't believe you. You're being chased through the primeval forest by an overly amorous gladiator, and all you can do is scold me for not being properly dressed." His green gaze slid purposefully over her body. "What exactly do you think you're wearing?"

As she glanced down at her gown, they heard the sharp crack of a branch breaking nearby. Putting a finger to his lips, he jerked his head, indicating the area immediately behind them. "Time to make our move," he whispered.

As silently as possible, they crept through the woods, away from the direction of the noise. When they had gone approximately a hundred yards, he paused and raised his head to listen. After several seconds, he was apparently satisfied that they could no longer be heard, because he grabbed Leah's hand and said, "Now we run like hell."

Which they did, as quickly as they could go in their bare feet. Leah had no idea where they were going, or what they would do when they got there. She simply allowed him to drag her along behind him. Almost at the same moment that she had decided she couldn't go an inch farther unless he threw her over his shoulder and carried her, he pulled her to a halt on the bank of a small stream.

Then a peculiar thing happened. Leah seemed somehow to split into two separate beings. She found she could view the two figures on the grass from some indeterminate spot above them. With unabashed interest, she studied the man kneeling beside the stream, admiring the bare, muscular chest that gleamed in the golden sunlight. The fluid lines of his body gave her a deep, real pleasure. Seconds later she frowned and became conscious of feeling exasperation toward the woman—herself—who lay on the grass beside him.

Instead of joining her in open admiration, this Leah was complaining.

"I'm tired, my feet are bruised, my knees are scraped and I have at least two thousand scratches on my legs," she muttered as she lay on her back, gasping for breath. "This doesn't make any kind of sense. I don't want to be here...and I wish I knew what in hell was going on."

He dipped his hand in the stream and bent down to splash water on his perspiring face and chest. "I assume we're in a dream."

"Yes, I did grasp that," she said irritably. "I've just never had a dream like this."

He turned toward her, his lips curving upward in a crooked smile. "Maybe it's my dream."

"No." She shook her head, instantly dismissing his suggestion. "No, if it's a dream, it's definitely mine. It was probably that cucumber. I know better than to have cucumber in my salad."

Giving a short bark of laughter, he flopped back on the grass, covering his face with one hand. "And if that's not a lowering thought, I've never heard one," he said in mock indignation. "The importance of my physical presence reduced to indigestion."

"That's another thing." She sat up, her stare an accusation. "If I'm going to dream your face, why am I dreaming someone else's personality?"

He propped himself on one elbow to look at her. "You've never dreamed about me before?"

"No, of course not," she said, frowning. The very idea shocked her. It seemed impertinent, somehow.

"I've dreamed about you," he said matter-of-factly.

"Well, what difference—" She broke off, eyeing him in open curiosity. "You dream about me?"

"All the time." He smiled. "But the dreams are usually... different from this one."

The idea that he dreamed of her was intriguing, even a little flattering. "Different? How?"

He raised one heavy, dark eyebrow, which gave him a slightly wicked appearance as he examined her body. Then suddenly, without any kind of hint to warn her, Leah's gown disappeared. One moment it was there, and the next she was naked.

The Leah who watched from a distance chuckled in gleeful amusement. What a silly woman, she thought. There was nothing in that body that should cause embarrassment. Her high, gently rounded breasts were the kind that inspired sculptors. The slender waist and long legs were perfectly formed—an opinion the man in the scene seemed to share as his gaze roamed Leah's body in open admiration. The Persian-lamp-shaped, rose-colored birthmark that rested low and slightly to the back of her left hip, rather than detracting from the loveliness, added to it—the Maker's stamp of approval.

Gasping, the Leah by the stream hastily crossed her arms over her bare breasts. Rising to her knees, she turned her back to him. "Put it back! Do you hear me? Mr. Gregory, I want my gown back!"

Before Leah could even blink, the two parts of her personality merged and the scene changed. She and Mr. Gregory now walked side by side along a cliff overlooking a deep, deserted stone quarry. She wore a long, flowing garment that seemed to be made of soft white linen. His was equally long, but looked like a blanket gathered and draped over an embroidered, short-sleeved tunic.

"How's that for service?" he asked, leaning down to adjust the strap on his sandal. "Not bad at all. A little drafty in places I'm not used to feeling a draft, but not bad." He glanced at her as he straightened. "Under the circumstances, maybe you'd better call me Paul."

"How did you do that?" she asked, her eyes narrowed, her voice suspicious.

"I didn't.... At least, I don't think I did. I liked things just exactly the way they were," he said, allowing his gaze to drift over her bare shoulder. "But you know how dreams are. You never know what to expect."

"Even if I knew 'how dreams are,' this is not like any dream I've ever heard about," she said helplessly. Then she suddenly stopped walking and looked out over the quarry. "Wait! I just thought of something," she said, turning to him eagerly. "Let's jump off."

He stared at her, his face blank. "Is it something I said?"

"No...no, listen." In her enthusiasm, she grasped his upper arm with both hands. "In dreams, when you fall, you always wake up before you hit the bottom. If we jump, we'll have to wake up." The neatness of the plan brought a smile of satisfaction to her lips.

"You're nuts." Now it was his turn to look suspicious. "Forget it. You can do what you want, but count me out." As she sputtered indignantly, he began walking again, talking to her over his shoulder. "People die in their sleep. And they can't come back to say, 'Hey, guess what? I finally hit bottom.' As I said, count me out. I have no intention of waking up dead tomorrow."

Leah made a face at his back. She hadn't thought of that. And she didn't like the fact that he had thought of it instead of her.

"So what do you suggest?" she asked, her voice disgruntled as she stepped gingerly around a pile of rocky debris, holding her long skirt out of the way with one hand.

The terrain had become rougher as they walked. Huge boulders of white rock rose beside them, blocking their view of the quarry.

"I suggest we play it out. In fact, that's all we can do. If people could arrange their dreams, there would be no nightmares," he added with maddening calm.

Together they skirted a large outcropping of rock...and walked squarely into a gathering of Roman soldiers.

And there was no doubt that they were soldiers. Their uniforms could never be mistaken for anything else. They had been in the process of passing around a goatskin wine bag, but the appearance of Leah and Paul caused an immediate and definite reaction. Several of the men pulled out swords; others pointed razor-sharp javelins threateningly in the direction of the intruders.

Leah swallowed heavily. "Play it out, you say?"

As the men began to advance, Paul swore under his breath. "Leah . . . honey, if you're going to wake up, now is the time to do it."

"Well, well, well," one of the soldiers said, eyeing Leah. "What have we here? A beauteous maid, I vow."

His British accent made the situation slightly ridiculous, but Leah had no time to play critic, she was too busy trying to hide behind Paul.

Seconds later, when she was grasped by several rough hands and dragged away from Paul, a low growling sound came from deep in his throat. Rage flashed in his green eyes, and his chest swelled as he drew a harsh breath. Then, without warning, he threw himself headlong into the middle of the soldiers who held her.

For a moment the Romans appeared startled and dropped back, almost in fear. But only for a moment. As soon as it dawned on them that they were six men—six armed men—against one, they met his anger enthusiastically and en masse.

An involuntary cry escaped Leah as Paul was caught on the chin by a chain-wrapped fist, then in the stomach, then on the side of the head. Each soldier seemed determined to take part. As Paul continued to stand against the violent blows, Leah felt time slow down, dragging out the scene interminably. She knew she was screaming at them, but she didn't know what words she used. Eventually she began to claim the pain as her own, flinching each time a blow was struck.

When at last he fell, most of the men stepped away, breathing heavily from their exertions. But two of the soldiers stayed behind. The fact that their laughter didn't sound particularly vicious or cruel as they kicked him in the back and the side made the scene even more unbearable.

"Paul!" she screamed, struggling against the hands that held her tightly. "Stop that! Damn it, you stupid cowards, let him go!"

The sound of her voice drew the two men's attention away from Paul. Giving one last kick each for good measure, they turned and moved in her direction, smiling at her in boyish good humor.

"Paul, are you all right?" she asked, panicking when he didn't move. "Paul?"

Slowly, painfully, he rolled to his knees, then rose to his feet, swaying slightly. "I'm fine," he said. His voice was thick and hoarse, as though speaking were an effort for him. Then he glanced over to where she stood. "They—" He broke off to draw a deep, raspy breath, then gave her a weak grin. "They wouldn't have beaten me so easily if I hadn't tripped over my skirt."

When he began to move toward her, the two men who had kicked him raised their iron-tipped spears, holding him at bay.

"Okay, chaps, you've had enough playtime."

The mocking comment came from a large, dark soldier with a deep scar on the side of his neck. Until that moment he had stood back against the outcrop of rocks, out of their line of sight. He was dressed like the other men: leather breastplate above a short white skirt and a red robe clasped at the neck and thrown back over both shoulders. But Leah realized immediately that he was not at all like them. Authority was in his every step.

The other men began to mutter, "The captain's here. Look, it's the captain," and moved automatically out of his way as he walked toward Leah.

"Now it's my turn," the captain said, grasping her chin to turn it toward him. "Nice . . . very nice."

"Wait a minute," Paul said loudly as he wiped the blood from his mouth. "I didn't have a chance, with half a dozen of you and only one of me. There's no challenge in that," he chided, shaking his head. "But—" he glanced at the man who still held Leah's chin, the man who was obviously the group's leader "—you . . . now *you* look like a sporting man. How about a race? I'll bet I could win a chariot race against you any day of the week."

"Cor," one of the soldiers whispered, his eyes widening. "The man's a bloomin' idiot."

The captain turned his head slowly and looked at Paul for several taut seconds. Then he threw back his head and gave a shout of laughter. "Alf's right; you're insane," he said, then turned back to Leah, who shrank instinctively from the look in his eyes.

"Well, of course, if you don't think you can beat me . . ." Paul said, shrugging.

When the other soldiers began to mutter among themselves, the leader's face grew purple with fury. Swinging around sharply, he walked to where Paul was being held and grasped his toga with one meaty fist. "No one can beat me in a chariot race!" he roared. *"No one!"*

"Put the beauteous maid where your mouth is," Paul said, his voice calm and unconcerned. "Winner takes all."

The captain glanced back toward Leah and hesitated for a moment, then clenched his teeth and said, "Done."

Leaving one man to guard her, the other soldiers whooped and laughed and, obviously considering the challenge worthy of celebration, began to pass around the wineskin again.

When the two chariots were lined up side by side on a dirt road nearby, Leah's guard moved toward the vehicle with the rest of the men, dragging her along with him.

She had by now stopped struggling against her captor. Paul was in charge, and she thanked her lucky stars. It was no use telling herself this was only a dream. It was no use saying the whole thing was a product of her warped psyche. Dream or not, psyche or not—Leah didn't want to think about what would have happened to them if Paul hadn't challenged the Roman captain.

The soldier guarding her reached out and grabbed the wineskin away from one of his companions. As soon as he tilted his head back to drink, Paul moved casually around the area until he stood beside her.

"How do you feel?" she asked, her brown eyes showing concern.

"Fine, I think." He moved his shoulder muscles tentatively, then raised one brow in surprise. "Not an ache or a bruise. This dream business isn't all bad."

She relaxed slightly. Then, studying the two chariots and the row of horses pawing the ground in front of them, she frowned and whispered, "Paul, I'm sure you know what you're doing—honestly, I don't doubt you for a minute—but . . . do you know how to drive one of those things?"

"Depends on whether it's automatic or standard shift," he said absently as he glanced from the crowd to the black chariot that was nearest them. "Look, Leah—" He broke off abruptly as the captain joined the group behind the chariots.

"I've put two men three kilometers down this road by the crooked oak tree," he told Paul. "When I reach it first, as I most certainly will, I'm going to pull over and beat the hell out of you for your insolence."

Paul chuckled, saluting sharply. Then, glancing over the captain's shoulder, his eyes widened in horror. "Oh, my God! Would you look at that!"

Everyone swung around, including Leah, which meant she wasn't prepared when Paul grabbed her around the waist and hauled her willy-nilly into one of the waiting chariots.

By the time the inebriated soldiers could react, Paul had whipped the four gray horses into a wild frenzy and he and Leah were speeding away in the sleek two-wheeled wagon.

After a stunned moment, Leah gave a victorious shout. The trees and small structures lining the road became a brown-and-green blur as the chariot traveled swiftly past. The wind whipped her face, and excitement sped through her bloodstream, causing her to laugh in sheer exhilaration. It was like nothing she had ever felt. It was like flying!

Suddenly a low noise intruded, and Leah's laughter died in her throat. The noise grew louder until it was a rumbling, thunderous sound that filled the air. Gripping Paul's waist tightly, she glanced over her shoulder.

It was not one chariot that followed them, but three, and several riders on horseback, every single one of them in ardent pursuit. And as she watched with wide eyes, the distance between them grew noticeably shorter.

"They're getting closer!" she shouted.

"Yes," he acknowledged. His voice was loud, but still as calm and steady as ever. "I think we might have ticked them off just a tad."

"A tad?" She rolled her eyes expressively at the understatement. "They're going to boil us in oil. Oh, but, Paul, you were *wonderful*." She pressed her face to his broad back, tightening her arms around his waist in an impulsive hug. Seconds later she raised her head again, standing on tiptoe to get closer to his ear. "What kind of stale trick was that, anyway? 'Oh, my

God, look.' It sounded like something from an old Crosby-Hope movie," she said, giggling helplessly.

"It's stale in the 1980s," he yelled back to her. "In Roman times it is probably fresh and new and different. Who cares? It worked, didn't it?"

"You're right. It doesn't—" As they rounded a tree-lined curve, she broke off with a panicky squeal.

There, in the middle of the road, a road with no shoulders and no passing lane and no off-ramp, was an ox-drawn cart overflowing with caged chickens.

"Oh, hell," Paul breathed in awe as he jerked back on the reins.

In the second before they collided with the cart, bells began to ring wildly, filling the air around them.

* * *

Leah groaned, her fingers fumbling blindly on the bedside table to find and turn off the alarm. When she succeeded only in knocking it to the floor, she pulled a pillow over her head to drown out the noise.

Then, slowly, she removed the pillow and sat up, her eyes still slightly unfocused from sleep.

What a crazy, freaked-out dream, she thought, resting her chin on her blanket-covered knees. A gurgle of husky laughter escaped her. Paul—no, Mr. Gregory, she corrected herself silently. Mr. Gregory in a Roman toga?

Only of course it hadn't been Mr. Gregory at all. Her subconscious had put his face—it was undoubtedly a compelling face—on a dream man. It was impossible for her to imagine the oh-so-stiff and oh-so-correct VP rescuing her from a band of drunken Roman soldiers.

Later, in the shower, she began to laugh again, remembering his expression when she had suggested jumping off a cliff, remembering the way he had wrestled with the toga to adjust the straps on his sandals. He had been funny and fascinating, this man her dreams had built.

Then, even later in the morning while she rushed around the bedroom gulping down a cup of coffee as she got ready for work, she cursed that man. He might have been fascinating, but that was no excuse for making her late.

At last she managed to pull herself together. She held a piece of toast between her teeth as she opened the door to leave. Then, abruptly, she stopped, frowning as she pulled the toast out of her mouth. Something was wrong. Glancing around the living room, she saw her briefcase lying on the coffee table. She had almost walked out without it. That had never happened to her before. Shaking her head ruefully, she quickly retrieved it.

Ordinarily Leah left for work early in order to avoid the murderous traffic on Central Expressway. Today, even though she was only fifteen minutes later than usual, it was bumper to bumper.

Move two inches and stop. Move two inches and stop. The frustrating rhythm continued the entire fifteen miles she had to travel to work.

By the time she reached the Universal building and found a parking place—at exactly three minutes to eight—the Roman dream was forgotten and the only thing on Leah's mind was getting her hands on a helicopter so she would never have to set tire to Central Expressway again.

Leah pushed the glass door aside, her heels clicking sharply on the marble floor as she headed for the group of people in front of the elevators. She shifted her shoulder bag restlessly and stared, along with everyone else, at the lights over the elevators, following the progress of each of them to determine which one to stand in front of.

Out of the corner of her eye she saw her boss standing several feet away and turned toward him, smiling politely. "Good morning, P—"

Leah broke off in dismay, quickly swallowing his first name. When he stared at her as though waiting for her to continue, she cleared her throat noisily. "Powerfully nice weather we're having, isn't it?" she substituted lamely.

Powerfully nice weather?

Quick thinking, Leah, she told herself with disgust as she stepped into the elevator along with a half-dozen other people. Once again the old glib tongue amazes with the power and swiftness of its rapier wit.

Mr. Gregory had looked at her as if she had had a few bricks missing. As well he might, she thought ruefully. She could have said anything. She could have said Pi-R-squared, or Pigs fly at night. Either one would have made more sense than what she had actually said. It was that stupid dream again, she told herself as she stalked into her office. First it had made her late; then it had tripped up her tongue.

By sheer determination she managed to put the incident and the dream that had caused it out of her mind. As soon as she became caught up in her work, it was easier. She had sent to Mr. Gregory's office the figures she had worked on the night before. When he didn't summon her to rake her over the coals, she assumed they were acceptable.

At one-thirty Leah was still leaning over her work, a sandwich in one hand, a pencil in the other. She glanced up when Charlotte walked in and stood in front of her desk.

"Mr. Gregory's secretary called." The tall, thin woman was slightly hesitant. "He wants you to go with him to DFW Airport to talk to Mr. Jacobs."

Leah wrinkled her nose thoughtfully. Carl Jacobs was Universal's local PR man. He was excellent at his job, and she had met with him often in the course of her work, but ordinarily he came to headquarters for meetings, not the other way around.

Leah nodded, her mind only partially on what Charlotte was saying as she looked down at her work and made a quick correction. "Did Norma say when he wanted to leave?" she mumbled through a bite of ham-salad sandwich.

"Now."

Leah glanced up, choking on her food, and Charlotte gave her a sympathetic smile. "She said he would meet you in the lobby in five minutes."

Sighing, Leah gave the sandwich a last, longing look, then dropped it back on the paper plate. After scooting back her chair, she stood and stepped into her shoes.

Thirty minutes later she and Mr. Gregory were in his car, heading west on the airport freeway. He had carefully explained what he wanted to accomplish, and since then neither of them had spoken.

No idle chitchat for the VP, she thought as she stared out the side window. Out of sheer boredom she began to read the billboards on the side of the freeway, concentrating on them as though they were world-class literature, studying them as though she hadn't seen them a thousand times before.

Fun in Hawaii. Paris in Spring. Budget Fare to the Orient. Their competitors' signs were singularly uninspiring, she thought, pleased that Universal had so far not seen fit to use that particular means of advertisement.

Then a billboard caught her eye, and she turned her head, staring at it until they were past. Experience the Glory That Is Still Rome, it read.

Rome, she thought, a small smile tugging at her lips. She had never been to Rome. If she went there now, would she find the countryside anything like what she had seen in that silly dream?

Shifting casually in her seat, she surreptitiously studied the man next to her. Was the man in her dreams really so much like Mr. Gregory? she wondered. Their features were very similar—but, no, the eyes weren't the same. These were set deeper, and the green was darker, without a hint of sparkle. Now that she looked more closely, the rest of his features were also different. Surely the man in her dream hadn't had this harsh, gaunt look. Yes, Mr. Gregory was definitely older than the man she had conjured in the middle of the night, she told herself in satisfaction.

"Is something wrong, Miss French?"

Leah blinked, then felt color rise in her cheeks. She was no longer being surreptitious. She was staring openly. It was no wonder he was giving her the Frown.

"I'm sorry," she said, her voice husky with embarrassment. "I—I had something on my mind."

"Are you sure? You were staring at me as though I were a piece of mold in a petri dish."

"No, no, really—"

"Is this trip an inconvenience for you?" One dark eyebrow was raised, as though daring her to make such a confession. "You had something more important on your schedule?"

Only a ham-salad sandwich, she thought, swallowing a nervous laugh. "I had nothing more important." To her surprise, she sounded perfectly composed. "I was simply distracted by my thoughts. If I seemed rude, I apologize."

Once again silence fell between them. Then, out of the blue, he said, "We had to leave right away in order to catch Jacobs before he left for an appointment. I want him to see the first section of the proposal today, because we need to start work on it tomorrow."

Leah listened to him with a blank expression on her normally vital face. He was actually offering her an explanation of his actions, she thought in astonishment. That was like God making a special trip down just to explain why He had created snails.

"Yes, of course," she said weakly.

They were halfway through the meeting with Carl Jacobs before Leah finally lost the stunned feeling her superior's unusual behavior had caused. After stunned, she switched to just plain awed.

One of the highlights of her job was watching Mr. Gregory work. On more occasions than she could count she had seen people openmouthed at his intelligence and immediate grasp of any problem connected with business. Today was no exception. This was the man she knew.

But it was more than that, she decided. As strange as it seemed, this was the man with whom she felt comfortable. She knew exactly where she stood with him. Feeling a relief that was completely out of proportion to the problem, Leah carefully placed her boss back in the neat little psychological pigeonhole she had built for him. Her mental pond could do without any more ripples on it.

After the meeting, as they approached the escalator that would take them from the mezzanine to the lobby, a small boy shoved his way eagerly in front of them. Leah smiled, but she didn't pay the child any particular attention because her mind was still on several points Carl had brought up.

Suddenly the boy seemed to lose his footing and pitched forward. For a terrible instant Leah froze. Then, before she could even begin to react, Mr. Gregory scooped the boy up and held him securely in his arms.

Leah let out a long breath of relief, suppressing a shudder. A plunge down the steep steps would have been painful, at the very least.

"I always have trouble with them, too," her boss said to the boy. "Moving steps. Moving sidewalks. Little boxes that float up and down in buildings. Do you suppose someday they'll invent newspapers that automatically move to our doorsteps so we won't have to hunt in the bushes for them?"

His voice wasn't so very different from what she was used to, but when Leah heard the boy giggle, she glanced at the man standing one step below her. His green eyes were sparkling with humor. She couldn't look away from them. When she saw him smile at the boy in his arms, she felt dizzy. She was glad they were at the bottom of the escalator, or she might have pitched downhill herself.

Almost immediately she realized that this wasn't the first time she had felt this way. It was the same kicked-in-the-stomach sensation she had had the first time she'd seen Paul Gregory—which meant Leah hadn't done quite as good a job as she had thought of burying the attraction she felt for him.

Leah's first reaction to this revelation was panic. Her second reaction was surprise at her first reaction.

Wariness or chagrin she could have understood, but panic?

The little boy's mother met them at the bottom and helped to dispel Leah's mood as she began to scold him for running away from her. Immediately Mr. Gregory was his normal self again, his face expressionless and somewhat forbidding. The smile and her reaction to it had both been so fleeting that Leah began to wonder if she had only imagined them.

By the time she returned to her apartment that night, she had managed to convince herself that her mind had indeed played tricks on her. Earlier, on the way to the meeting, she had studied Mr. Gregory intensely, searching for a resemblance to the man in her dreams. And eventually her mind had let her see exactly what she had been looking for.

When a group of faithful observers stood around waiting for a statue to cry, eventually they saw it happen. What had happened to her was obviously based on the same principle.

Did that mean she wanted to see a softer, more human side of her boss? she asked herself, then immediately shook her head in a vigorous motion.

"No way," she muttered aloud. The attraction she felt was totally illogical, some kind of crazy physical thing that was best ignored.

"Just watch out, Leah," she told herself wryly. "If you aren't careful you'll be the leading candidate for associate vice president of public relations in a funny farm."

She dawdled as she prepared for bed, glancing over her shoulder occasionally at the bed. For half an hour she sat in the chair across the room from her bed and thumbed through several *National Geographic*s. Finally, mentally girding her loins, she crawled under the covers, clutching the edges as she pulled them up around her neck. For a while she merely lay there with her eyes wide open. Then, tentatively, she closed them and waited to see what would happen.

Nothing. No dreams, no drunken Romans, no chariot races. Relaxing with a sigh, she snuggled down comfortably.

The next morning the only dream Leah could remember from the night before had had to do with her promotion. The job had been given to one of the giant pandas in the Washington zoo. Vaguely she remembered protesting the action, stating in court that it was a clear case of sexual discrimination because the position of associate VP had been given to Hsing-Hsing instead of Ling-Ling. Although the dream had been crazy, it was a normal kind of craziness. The kind of craziness Leah could handle.

Gradually, over the next two weeks, Leah stopped thinking about the Roman dream. Although she could pull up any detail with perfect clarity, she definitely didn't wish to recall it. She put in her ten hours a day at work, went out on a couple of dates and stubbornly avoided thinking about Mr. Gregory.

Preparations for the campaign continued to run smoothly, even when Mr. Gregory went out of town for several days on company business. As could be expected, while the cat was away, the other mice in the building played. But in the midst of the *en fête* atmosphere, Leah worked even harder. She was too close to her promotion to slack off now. And she was determined that no dumb male panda would get *her* job.

One morning when she walked into the building she knew instantly that her boss had returned. Solid, sober industriousness reigned as far as the eye could see. Once again Captain Bligh was at the helm of his ship.

Predictably he had brought work with him. Early on the day of his return, he sent down two huge files with a curt note asking for a reorganization of the original proposal to allow for new data he had obtained on his trip.

Leah stayed at the office until seven-thirty that evening, then scooped up the rest of her work to take home.

At the apartment her routine was the same as always, except that tonight she substituted clam chowder for the salad and forgot to turn on her answering machine. She was only momentarily interrupted when David Yarrow, a man she dated occasionally, called to chat. A fellow workaholic, he knew by her distracted tone that she was buried in business and didn't keep her.

It was fifteen minutes past midnight when Leah glanced up at the buzzing television and began to massage with both hands the aching muscles in her neck.

Only a half hour's work to go, she thought wearily. Only half an hour, and then she could go to bed. That was the good news. The bad news was that she wasn't sure she could hold up for another thirty minutes. Her back was stiff from bending over the coffee table, and her eyes burned from staring so long at the reports.

She leaned back against the soft cushions of the couch. Maybe she would rest her eyes for just a second, she thought. For just one second . . .

Chapter Three

How now, spirit! whither wander you?

A Midsummer Night's Dream—Act II, Scene 1

As Leah strolled along the crowded street, she pulled the raccoon collar of her wool coat closer around her face. For a while, as she walked, she simply stared at the people passing her on the sidewalk. On the corner, under a streetlamp that cast inadequate light in the early evening hours, a newsboy hawked papers from a bundle on the sidewalk. His worn coat was open to show the suspenders that held up patched brown knickers.

"Dempsey to face Tunney in rematch!" he shouted, holding a newspaper high in the air. "Extra! Extra! Dempsey to face Tunney in rematch!"

"Not again," Leah murmured, rolling her eyes in resigned exasperation. Then she turned her head sharply, almost swallowing her gum in the process, to watch a car as it passed on the street.

"Rumble seats, knickers, spats—what a kick," she said, shaking her head.

At least this time she wasn't wearing her night-gown, she thought in relief. And that wasn't the only difference. Even though the sights and sounds were slightly confusing, Leah knew where she was going.

When she caught sight of a gray stone building a block ahead, her steps quickened. As she reached the building, she passed the steps leading up to the insurance company that rented all three floors and took the steps that led down to the basement.

Seconds after she knocked on the heavy metal-clad wooden door, a small hatch swung inward. From her angle all Leah could see was a bulbous red nose that leaned determinedly sideways. She stood, vigorously chewing the peppermint-flavored gum as she waited. A moment later the peephole closed and the door opened.

"Hi, Leah," the large gray-haired man said, his words slow and slightly slurred from too many years of illegal, bare-knuckle boxing.

"Hiya, Pops," she said pertly, swinging past him. Then her steps faltered.

Hiya, Pops?

Heaven help me, she thought, choking on a dismayed laugh. She sent silent notice to whoever or whatever was orchestrating this dream that she refused to say twenty-three skiddoo. That was above and beyond the call of duty.

"Well, hell-*o*, kiddo."

Turning her head, she smiled at the two men coming up behind her. They both carried instrument cases and wore turtleneck sweaters with their knickers.

"Hello, Artie...Bert." She batted her eyelashes, then continued walking, squealing in laughing protest when one of them slapped her on the rear.

After opening the third door on the left, she entered a small dressing room containing a chaise longue that had probably once been white, a wooden coatrack that leaned drunkenly to one side, a mirrored vanity and a scarred, doorless wardrobe that held a variety of glittering costumes.

She stripped off her coat and hung it on the coatrack, then walked to the mirrored vanity. Slowly, carefully, she studied her face. Giving a low, breathless laugh, she pulled off the brown cloche and shook her hair free. A smooth fringe of blond bangs fell straight across her forehead, and the back was neat and boyishly short. On her lips bright red lipstick gleamed. Her eyelids were heavily made up, and her false eyelashes were outrageously long.

"Good Lord," she murmured, taking the gum out of her mouth to hold it gingerly between two fingers. "I look...I look—" She cocked her head to one side and grinned. "I look kind of cute. Not exactly Zelda Fitzgerald, but cute." With that she popped the gum back in her mouth.

There was a sharp knock on the door. "Thirty minutes, Miss French."

"Thanks, Johnny," she called out, and began to strip off her clothes.

She was braless beneath the straight lilac dress. Instead, she wore what looked like a sleeveless undershirt and cotton bloomers. When she had removed the underwear, she slipped into a long white satin robe and sat down to redo her makeup for the harsh glare of spotlights, her movements practiced and efficient.

Twenty minutes later she stood in satin bloomers, garter belt and silk stockings. Reaching into the wardrobe, she pulled out a swirl of sapphire-blue chiffon. The beaded bodice of the dress was cut low and straight across, leaving her shoulders bare except for three silver straps on each side. The dress had no shape of its own until it reached just below her hips, then it flared out, ending in a handkerchief hemline that occasionally showed a glimpse of silk-clad knee when she moved. The matching beaded headdress fitted close to her head, covering her hair completely, and had a delicate fringe that framed her face like silver rain.

Leah had just stepped into her shoes when Johnny called the five-minute warning.

She pulled open the door to her dressing room and walked to the side entrance of the stage. The band was playing a hot, jazzy Gershwin tune. As she stood waiting, she felt her stomach tighten into familiar knots of tension.

Suddenly the lights in the club dimmed and an obese tuxedo-clad man stepped up to the microphone. "Okay—okay, calm down," he said to the audience with a chuckle. "We won't make you suffer any longer. Now...the moment you've been waiting for...our own—*Leah French!*"

When the spotlight swung in her direction, Leah stepped onto the stage. Loud applause and enthusiastic shouts greeted her. Looking out over the smoky club, she smiled and threw the audience kisses until the noise died away.

The band began to play behind her and, right on cue, she went into her song. It startled her to hear the low, sultry sound of her own voice. Somewhere in the back of her mind, she knew she couldn't carry a tune. But tonight she could. And she carried it very well as she sang the soft love song. Every word was exactly right, as though she had rehearsed dozens of times.

The excitement in the nightclub reached her, spurring her on as she reached the last lingering note. After a brief, electric moment, the room erupted with applause. Shouts of "Atta girl, Leah!" mingled with the more sophisticated "Brava!" reflecting the mixed audience. The top of society sat next to the working class. Speakeasies were very democratic, Leah thought with a smile.

Before the applause died away the band swung into a bouncy number filled with sexual innuendo. The lyrics and the coy, slightly naughty expression on her face as she sang brought enthusiastic hoots and loud laughter.

For almost an hour Leah sang. Then, just as she began her last number, she spotted him at the bar, and her heart jerked in her chest.

As she sang, Leah let her gaze drift over the dark, slicked-back hair, the hawk-like nose, the broad shoulders whose power even the elegant tuxedo couldn't hide and the narrowed, piercing green eyes. She stared, and felt as though she were looking at her lover.

Then suddenly she knew that was exactly what she was doing. She was staring at the man who was her lover. And she also knew that she had been unconsciously looking for him since the minute she walked on stage.

I remember you, she thought, sending a silent message across the room. *I remember you well, my love.*

Scenes and emotions flashed through her mind. Cold champagne and warm, naked flesh pressed close to hers. Stolen nights away from the excitement and bright lights that she had once thought were all-important to her. Vitality and strength rippling beneath her urgent fingertips. Long, slow walks down a country road. Her body being pressed down into the softness of fallen leaves. Achingly beautiful moments. Moments of desperate need.

Sweet heaven, she thought, her heart swelling with pride. With his looks he could have any woman he wanted, but he wanted her.

Then she blinked twice. No, she told herself in confusion. This was Mr. Gregory. Vice president...

Vulcan...the Frown...Captain Bligh...Universal Air. But no matter how hard she tried to deny it, she knew she was tied in some way to the man at the bar.

Turning back to the rest of the audience, she put everything she had into the remainder of the song. When she finished, the applause was simply noise to her. It no longer had the power to thrill her. Only one thing, one man, could do that now. Smiling and waving to the audience, she returned her gaze eagerly to the bar.

He was gone.

At some time during the song he had left. Her bottom lip trembled slightly as a deep emptiness took hold of her. The spotlight faded, and in darkness she turned and moved off the stage. She felt drained and weary as she walked down the hall and opened the door of her dressing room.

When the door closed softly but firmly behind her, Leah spun around in a startled movement. And before she could even say his name, he had pulled her into his arms. His lips found hers instantly, and there was nothing tentative about the kiss. Undisguised hunger and deep need were expressed in every movement. His tongue probed urgently, taking her breath away, shocking her with its familiarity.

I can't, she thought in panic as she began to pull away. "No—don't," she murmured. "We can't—you don't know what you're doing."

"What the hell, Leah," he coaxed, his voice deep and husky, his breath warmly enticing on her lips. "It's only a dream. Go with it."

It's a dream, she repeated silently, testing the thought. It was only a dream. Her growing need urged her to accept the premise. Yes, she thought eagerly as she melted against him. Yes, it's only a dream.

With a groan, his restless mouth moved to her throat. "I've been wanting to do this for so long," he said in a rough whisper. "Every time you walked into my office—so efficient, so distant, so damn beautiful—I had to fight to keep from pulling you into my arms and throwing you down on the couch."

The feel of his mouth on her neck sent excitement shivering through her body. "What office?" she murmured, grasping his shoulders to keep him close.

"Who knows?" He cupped both her breasts, pushing upward so that the rounded flesh swelled above the top of her dress. "Who in hell cares?" he added as he pressed his mouth to her trembling softness.

His breathing grew harsh and quick as he pulled her down with him onto the chaise longue. His hunger for a touch, a kiss, seemed to be as compelling as her own. When she undid several buttons of his white silk shirt and pushed one hand inside, his muscles tensed instantly: then he shuddered and covered her hand with his, pressing it closer to his heated flesh.

"Leah—oh, Leah," he murmured hoarsely as he pulled her tightly against him.

She glanced up, studying his face. Raising his hand, he outlined her lips with one finger. "You look stunned," he whispered.

She nodded slowly. "I feel stunned. Stunned...and a little silly."

"Silly?"

"I didn't know false eyelashes were so heavy...and awkward," she said, smiling up at him. "I feel as if I'm bumping into you with them."

His chuckle had a deep, rich sound. "At first, when I realized there was enough oil on my hair to keep the New York subways running for a week, I felt silly, too."

Her answering laugh was hesitant and slightly breathless. "But not now?"

"No." His voice was clipped and intense as he pushed the silver straps from her shoulder and leaned down to test the smooth flesh with his lips. "No, silly is not what I feel at all," he whispered harshly.

Her eyelids drifted down, her head dropping back weakly as she savored the sensation of his mouth on her body. She felt his touch in every pore, on every square inch of her flesh. It became a part of her, as necessary to her existence as the air she breathed.

Suddenly, behind them, the door crashed against the wall as it was thrown violently open. Leah pushed herself away from Paul and jumped to her feet, quickly straightening her dress. Behind her, Paul stood slowly, with deliberation. They both stared at the two large men in black pin-striped suits who stood in front of the doorway.

"Charlie...Ed," she gasped, raising a hand to her throat as her heart began to pound.

The two men moved apart, leaving a gap between them that revealed a third man. Although he was not much more than five feet tall, confidence and power emanated from every inch of the newcomer. In the corner of his mouth, a fat cigar was clamped tightly between his teeth. His expression was calm and steady as he chewed on the cigar and stared at Leah. His smooth, unattractive face was known to every character, major or minor, in the Chicago underworld.

It was Louie the Lump.

Walking slowly to the vanity, he put his cigar out in a jar of cold cream. "Hello, Leah," he said, ignoring Paul. "Betcha didn't expect to see me tonight."

"Louie," she said weakly, "No—no, I didn't. I thought you were out of town."

"I got back this morning and decided to catch your show. It was great.... You got class, baby." He paused for a brief, chilling second, and his lips curved upward in a smile. "You also been cheatin' on me—with Mr. Fancy Pants here. That ain't nice, Leah. Did you forget who owns you? I bought you with a movie contract and a diamond necklace." He paused. "It was a fair deal. And what Louie buys stays bought. If it don't, Louie gets very unhappy. And you know what happens when Louie is unhappy."

Without glancing at his two large, silent employees, without changing his pleasant expression, Louie said quietly, "Shoot him."

Leah's mouth went dry with fear. "Louie—Louie, you can't do this. Listen to me, you can't shoot him. He's my boss."

The breathless statement brought a frown to Louie's wide lips. "You saying he bought my club without my knowing about it?"

"No—no, he's not my boss here," she stammered, moistening her lips nervously as she stared at Louie. "At Universal Air—never mind, it doesn't matter. You just can't do this to him. I'm the one who's been cheating on you, Louie. It's me you should shoot, not Paul."

"Shut up, Leah," Paul said sharply.

She glanced at him for a long moment, the desperation of her love showing in her brown eyes. Then she turned back to Louie. "I'll do anything you want me to—I won't ever see him again. I promise, Louie."

His laugh was not a pleasant sound. "That's right, sugar, you won't. Not unless you want to swim to the bottom of Lake Michigan. Because that's where your man's gonna be in an hour. Right down on the bottom, with little fishes feeding on his . . . eyeballs."

He glanced at the two men and gave a short nod.

Charlie and Ed pulled guns from under their coats and leveled them at Paul. As she watched helplessly, Leah felt perspiration break out on the palms of her hands. The next few seconds seemed to drag out for a small eternity. At the last moment, at the moment when she saw tension in Ed's hand, she threw herself in front of Paul.

She heard him shout, "No—*Leah!*" Then hot, piercing pain seemed to jerk her backward, into her lover's arms.

* * *

It was only after Leah's third cup of coffee that the dull, hung-over feeling began to fade. Her neck was stiff from sleeping on the couch, and she had probably caught cold because she hadn't turned down the air conditioning.

That stupid, stupid dream, she thought, gazing into her coffee as though mesmerized. It had been even worse than the first one. Leah hadn't even fought this time. She had simply gone along with it.

"And on top of that, I probably blew a movie contract," she muttered, pushing her chair back and standing.

Later, as she gave her long blond hair a light touch of hair spray, she stared at her face in the mirror. For a moment bright red lips and false eyelashes were superimposed over her own image.

She shook her head in irritation, pushing the vision away. "I don't want to think about what it meant," she told herself aloud for the third time that morning. "I don't want to think about Freud and his sneaky little theories about wish fulfillment."

Stalking into the living room, she picked up her briefcase and purse. "I simply want to have nice, normal dreams about stalking madmen and walking into the office naked," she added, her frustration almost comical as she slammed the door on her way out.

By midmorning, although she hadn't forgotten her adventures in the Roaring Twenties, she had managed to summon up enough humor to laugh at them.

Louie the Lump? she thought, giggling as she bent over her work. It was as ridiculous as her being a gun moll, or Mr. Gregory being a Fitzgerald-style playboy.

One thing Leah avoided thinking about was the scene with her boss in the small dressing room. Every time it flashed into her mind she felt heat rising in her face. And other places, she admitted ruefully. She disliked the thought that she was secretly sexually frustrated, and that those frustrations were causing the disturbing dreams.

She frowned in irritation. This silent debate was getting her nowhere, she decided obstinately. She would be better off forgetting the entire thing.

Which, of course, was easier said than done. At lunch Leah, Bitty and Shelley decided to try a Chinese restaurant that had recently opened nearby. They easily found a table in the half-empty dining room and got down to the main purpose of the luncheon: gossip.

Leah had never considered gossip a female occupation. She considered it a human one, and as long as it didn't turn malicious, she enjoyed listening, simply because she was intrigued by her fellow human beings.

"Have you seen Faith's new man?" Bitty asked as they handed the menus back to the waiter.

"What *is* this?" Leah asked. She gingerly picked up something from the appetizer plate the waiter had brought with the menus.

"It's an egg roll," Shelley said, grabbing one and taking an enthusiastic bite. As she chewed her expression grew bewildered. "No—no, it's definitely not an egg roll," she gasped, reaching frantically for a glass of water.

The other two women dropped the things back on the plate, mentally crossing the restaurant off their lists.

"What were you saying about Faith?" Leah asked.

"She's dating a guy from the mail room. I know you've seen him—tall and thin, with three-inch-thick glasses. His name is Derek."

Leah shook her head thoughtfully. "No, I can't remember seeing him. Is he okay?"

Shelley smiled. "The best he'll ever be is okay. But Faith is crazy about him. He sends her poetry on the back of transfer slips."

"Well...that's sort of romantic," Leah said doubtfully. "How long has it been going on?"

"Only about a week," Bitty said. "But don't worry. Neither of them is the type for heavy passion. Besides, Faith said she's not sure he's the One."

All three women groaned. "She'll never learn," Shelley said. "She's still looking for someone who'll sacrifice a kingdom for her."

"If any sacrificing is done, she'll be the one to do it," Leah said regretfully.

"Are you going to lecture her again?" Bitty asked with a grin. "Tell her all about how women degrade themselves by giving up too much for LOVE in capital letters?"

Sacrificing for love? Leah thought with an inward groan as she avoided her friend's eyes. They would laugh themselves silly if she told them about her dream of the night before.

Why on earth had she dreamed something like that? she wondered. She couldn't blame it all on sexual frustration. The tone had been too sickly sentimental. No one in his right mind would ever call her sentimental.

She frowned. She remembered reading somewhere that a cynic was nothing more than a disillusioned romantic. Was that it? Was it possible that the discarding of her adolescent fantasies had not been the natural product of maturing? Could it be that they had been discarded in self-defense after what had happened to her in college?

Leah hadn't thought of Grady in years, and it surprised her that he should enter her mind now. She didn't like the idea that her experience of a young love gone bad could still be affecting her after all this time.

As the talk flowed between the other two women, Leah contributed a word now and then, but her mind was taken over by her thoughts of the past.

She had been so young and innocent back then. Young and innocent and incredibly stupid.

It had been her first time away from home, and she'd found herself caught up in the excitement and scariness of moving into a sorority house and finally being her own person. She had met Grady on campus the second week of the term, and she had fallen in love with him the very same day. Gloriously, overwhelmingly, wholeheartedly in love, as only an eighteen-year-old can be.

Without hesitation, Leah had given one hundred and fifty percent to the budding relationship. She did

Grady's history research; she did Grady's laundry; she had even tried to change her personality so that she would be more like the person Grady wanted her to be.

Then, six months after she had met him, she had discovered that her True Love was sleeping with her roommate. And her best friend. And her English professor. The only person Grady wasn't sleeping with was Mrs. Ostley, her housemother, and at the time Leah had even wondered if the sweet, gray-haired lady hadn't spent an inordinate amount of time staring at Grady's tight jeans.

Leah shook her head. No, she refused to believe that an immature jerk like Grady had had a lasting affect on her life. But she wasn't a cynic. Not really. She was merely more objective than most women. There was nothing wrong with that, she told herself defensively.

And she kept telling herself that. In a few days she had the argument down pat. Working around Mr. Gregory helped enormously. He would have annihilated anyone without a tough shell.

As though to prove that the glimpse of the softer man Leah had seen at DFW had indeed been the figment of an overstimulated brain, her superior had been even more difficult to please. People had taken to ducking into rest rooms and janitors' closets when they saw him coming.

On an evening three days after her lunch with Bitty and Shelley, Leah sat in Mr. Gregory's office, her expression harried as she riffled through the papers in her lap.

"I'll get Leonard to check this out," she said.

"Make damned sure he goes to the right people. I won't have Posner messing it up at this stage of the game." He raised his gaze to hers, his lips tightening into the Frown. "He's your responsibility." Without giving her a chance to respond, he glanced at his watch. "It's seven-thirty. Get your things together and we'll go eat."

And then I can hear for another hour about all the things I've done wrong, she thought with silent sarcasm. She opened her mouth to make an excuse, but again she didn't get a chance to speak.

"If we can figure out what's going on with Maxwell," he said, standing to shrug into his jacket, "it could save us a lot of grief later on."

Leah gave an inward sigh of defeat when she realized there was no alternative to having dinner with him. She should have known better. Paul Gregory didn't make requests; he issued orders.

As she followed behind him in her own car, she reluctantly admitted that they did need to get the issue settled. Leon Maxwell, one of the key men from the advertising agency that had submitted the best proposal—not to mention the highest price—was giving off strange signals. Signals that were making everyone involved in the project uneasy. If Maxwell decided to play musical chairs and leave the agency now or anytime in the near future, it would throw a definite kink in the progress of the new promotional campaign.

In the dimly lighted steak house, they were ushered to a booth at the back of a large, elegantly subdued dining room. As soon as the waiter had taken their orders, Mr. Gregory turned back to Leah.

"Okay, tell me again exactly what Maxwell said to you—word for word," he said briskly.

She was still talking when their food arrived. And twice, as she ate, she had to reach into her briefcase for additional information.

Finally he nodded. "All right, that's it, then. Tomorrow I'll go see him myself—unofficially."

Leah relaxed against the leather seat with a sigh. She couldn't even remember what she had eaten. The wine, however, was excellent, she thought as she picked up her glass again. In the shadows left by the candles, it looked deep purple, almost black.

"This is a nice place," she murmured absentmindedly, momentarily letting down her guard. "But I don't know why restaurants with really excellent food insist on candlelight. I can never tell if I'm eating the appetizer or the flower arrangement."

She just happened to glance up as she finished speaking and was thereby witness to the most extraordinary change. The flickering light picked up a green sparkle in eyes that crinkled at the corners seconds before he leaned back in the seat and laughed.

Mr. Gregory laughed.

He actually laughed. A chuckle alone should have been, in Leah's opinion, accompanied by claps of thunder and flashes of lightning from heaven. But an honest-to-God laugh was inconceivable.

Good Lord, she thought, her brown eyes dazed, the man is gorgeous. The change in him was unreal. His features were softer, fuller. It looked as though he had discarded ten years in a single instant.

"What's wrong?" he said, still smiling as Leah stared in amazement.

"Nothing," she said, shaking her head helplessly. "I've just never seen you laugh before."

He raised one brow, his green eyes filled with amusement. "Well, Miss French, since I've never heard you say anything funny before, I guess we're even."

Never in a million years, she thought wryly. Not even if he left half his brain at home.

Picking up her glass, she swallowed the remainder of the wine in a single gulp. She felt strangely disoriented. This was not the man she had worked with for four years. This was a man she didn't know.

Then a crazy thought flashed through her mind. *But you do know him. This is the man who walks through your dreams.*

Chapter Four

Yet mark'd I where the bolt of Cupid fell:
It fell upon a little western flower—

A Midsummer Night's Dream—Act II, Scene 2

The radio spots stink."

Leah glanced at Mr. Gregory. They were in his car on their way back from a presentation at the advertising agency. It had been three weeks since he had taken her to the steak house for dinner, and although he occasionally relaxed enough to smile, he was still as formidable as ever.

"I know damn well those weren't Maxwell's work," he continued. "And he knows I know it. He was watching me too closely while they were being presented."

"Yes, I noticed," she said.

Universal's marketing department handled ads in the trade papers, and they usually took care of the daily newspapers and radio spots. But the media advertising for this particular campaign was tied together, which meant that the ad agency was responsible for newspaper, radio and television material.

"When I talked to Maxwell last week," Leah continued, "he hinted that someone in his office was trying to play politics, but at the time, he didn't seem to think it would affect us."

"It won't affect us," Mr. Gregory said, his features tight and hard. "I won't let it. No one plays games with Universal. If they can't straighten out their act, we'll pull the whole thing."

"The whole project?" Leah asked, frowning. "But that means it would be well into next year before we got it put together."

"They won't let us pull it," he said confidently. He pulled the car off the freeway and parked in front of a small restaurant. "I want you on this as soon as we get back to the office." As he stepped from the car, he was still talking, and Leah had to scramble out to catch his words. "Drop a few hints that Mr. Gregory thinks maybe he's given them too much leeway and just might start making suggestions."

She chuckled softly. He was right. They wouldn't have to pull the project. There was nothing an advertising man liked less than a client who tried to do his job for him.

For the next half hour they ate in silence. She could almost see his mind speeding through the problem, finding alternatives, testing and discarding ideas.

He met her gaze. "I think you'd better look over the campaign they did for us two years ago."

Leah remembered the campaign well. Although she hadn't been closely involved in the project, she had followed every step, absorbing it all so that when she had her chance she would be aware of the pitfalls.

"It was good stuff," he continued. "Study all the old copy and make notes. There was something there that's missing in this new material."

Leah nodded. That meant she would have to take the material home with her. She had three meetings scheduled for this afternoon—meetings she couldn't possibly put off.

A small frown tugged at her lips as she suddenly wondered if he knew how often she took work home with her. And if he knew, did he care?

She glanced up at his thoughtful, distant face. *Do you see me, Mr. Gregory? Do you really know who's sitting across the table from you?*

It annoyed her that she had even allowed the thought to develop. It shouldn't matter whether he saw her or not. But somehow, it did. It mattered very much.

She had never worked as closely with him as she had in the last two months. Now they stayed late at the office together. They shared meals. Breakfast, lunch, dinner—whatever was going at the time. On some days she spent more time with him in his office than she did in her own.

And never once had he even hinted that he saw her as an individual. As a woman.

Aha! she thought with derision. Now we're getting to the heart of the matter. She wanted him to see her as a woman.

Admit it, Leah, she goaded herself silently. You're annoyed because the man hasn't made a pass at you. You don't care if he doesn't see you as an individual. But your feminine ego demands that he see you as a woman. And that, may I say, is totally unworthy of you.

She tried to tell herself that she was relieved that he didn't notice her femininity. And logically, she knew she wouldn't even be thinking along these lines if the dreams hadn't made her take a closer look at him. They had forced her to accept him as a human being as well as her boss. She had begun to see that Paul Gregory wasn't the one-dimensional, characterless creature she had wanted him to be. He might not be the man in her dreams, but now she knew he was very definitely a man.

A man who didn't find her particularly attractive, she added silently. Even if it wasn't logical, even if it wasn't worthy of her, that fact bothered her more than she cared to think about.

Leah's smile was slightly acid. She would be in a terrible predicament if he ever decided to press for a more personal relationship, because then she would have to find a diplomatic way of turning him down.

But at least he could have had enough sensitivity to give her the opportunity of telling him no, she thought with total disregard for logic.

"Well?"

She looked up to find him staring at her in irritation. "I'm sorry," she murmured. "What did you say?"

"I asked you to come to my office before eleven tomorrow so we can discuss your impressions of the two projects." He spoke slowly and carefully, so that even someone of her limited intelligence could understand.

"Yes, of course," she said, feeling as thoroughly chastened as he had intended her to.

From that high point the day slid rapidly downhill. At four that afternoon she had just settled behind her desk after a thoroughly disorganized meeting when Charlotte buzzed her.

"Yes?" Leah said briskly.

"David Yarrow's on line two. Do you want me to tell him you're busy?" Charlotte's voice squeaked slightly, a sign of nerves. The brunette hated trying to put anyone off and would usually stammer for five minutes before putting the call through anyway.

Leah opened her mouth to tell the other woman that she couldn't take any calls; then she stopped. Maybe this was exactly what she needed. She rarely dated during the week, and tonight she had the extra work that Mr. Gregory had given her. But David had called at the right moment—or perhaps it was the wrong moment. She was still smarting from her boss's unconscious rejection of her femininity. A few hours with an attractive man—a man who left no doubt that he saw her as a woman—might be just what Leah needed to get her ego back in shape.

"I'll take the call," she said before she could change her mind.

At six-thirty that evening she met David in the parking lot of a small dinner club. "I can only stay a couple of hours," she said over her shoulder as she led the way into the club. "I have to work tonight."

"A couple of hours with you is better than a weekend with any other woman," he said earnestly, then grinned. "Besides, I have to get back to the studio by nine-thirty."

Leah laughed. David was a local television news reporter. He had been in the Dallas area for only two years but his blond curls, boyish grin and quick wit had already caused a perceptible rise in the ratings for his station's nightly news broadcast.

Immediately she began to relax. There were no undercurrents between them. No complications. The look in his gray eyes was basic. It said that she was an attractive, intelligent woman, and his job for the next two hours would be to enjoy that fact. He kept her amused with a constant flow of anecdotes about the people he had met in his work.

The two hours Leah had allotted for dinner flew by too quickly. Before she knew it, they were walking toward her car in the parking lot.

David opened the car door for her, leaning on it as he gazed down at her. "The mayor's giving a party next Friday," he said. He placed a companionable hand on her neck, massaging it gently. "Want to come with me?"

She smiled. "Let me check my schedule and get back to you."

"Do that," he murmured, then lowered his head, his lips finding hers in a warm kiss.

Leah sighed and leaned toward him. It was a nice kiss from a nice man, and she was just beginning to really enjoy it when suddenly she pulled away, frowning.

"I'd better get going," she said, avoiding his eyes. "Work—I have to get that work done." She swallowed nervously, trying to get her brain to function as she slid into the driver's seat. "It was wonderful seeing you again, David.... I owe you a dinner."

She didn't look at him as she shut the door and started the car, but as she pulled out of the parking lot, she glanced in the rearview mirror. He was still standing there, staring after her.

He must have thought she had lost her mind. Maybe she had. That was the only explanation she could find at the moment for her behavior. For a moment, for one brief second as David kissed her, she had felt guilty. *Guilty!*

As she drove, her hands gripped the steering wheel tightly, her thoughts spinning. The whole thing was crazy. Why should she feel guilty about kissing an attractive, likable man? Was some long-buried hang-up finally rising to the surface?

That was totally unreasonable, she told herself. She didn't have any hang-ups about men. It was only a friendly kiss, for Pete's sake. She had kissed dozens of men, and nothing like this had ever happened before.

So what in hell was wrong with her? she wondered in confusion.

Even when she was in front of the television with her work spread out on the coffee table, the feeling nagged at her, pulling her thoughts away from the campaign.

Luckily, the differences Mr. Gregory had told her to look for were glaringly obvious. The movie hadn't finished playing when she pulled it out of the VCR and walked to her bedroom.

She sat on the edge of the bed, stretching her back. No more thinking, she ordered herself firmly. No thoughts of unfounded, random guilt. No thoughts of the two campaigns. Tomorrow was soon enough to think about it all.

She plumped her pillow, then lay back and closed her eyes. Seconds later her eyelids began to twitch gently.

* * *

Leah stood in a small, open valley that rested between gently rolling hills. Around her, wildflowers made a vivid rainbow for her to pass through. Her sunbonnet rested on her back, exposing the blond hair that gleamed in the bright spring sunlight. The faded blue calico of her dress pressed against her legs as she walked through the knee-high growth.

Her arms were overflowing with pink and red and yellow blooms. She had enough flowers for every room of their small ranch house, but still she was reluctant to start back. It was spring, the sun was shining, the breeze was warm on her face and she was young. That was enough reason for dawdling.

Laying aside her bundle of flowers, she sat down, then flung out her arms and flopped back on the soft grass. She closed her eyes and inhaled deeply. A couple of months from now the grass would be stiffer and the air would be dryer. But now it was spring, and she could imagine no more perfect place on the earth.

She opened her eyes as the sound of hoofbeats reached her. Sitting up, she turned toward the noise and saw a horse as it topped the small hill to her right. Leah shaded her eyes with one hand, studying the rider. Surely Pa hadn't sent one of the men after her? she thought. She hadn't been gone more than two hours.

But when the rider drew closer, she knew it wasn't one of the men from the ranch. She felt her muscles tighten in surprise and scrambled to her feet. The rider pulled his horse to a halt several yards from her and stepped from the saddle in a fluid movement.

Leah felt a wave of emotion wash over her, its force making her sway slightly. Suddenly she began to run toward him. He met her halfway and grabbed her up in his arms, swinging her around in a joyous circle, as though he too felt the power of being young on a spring day.

"Paul," she whispered breathlessly. "When did you get back?"

"Today," he said, laughing down at her. Sparks of platinum light appeared in his green eyes.

When he set her on her feet, she pulled away from him, and her golden-brown eyes dropped in embarrassment and confusion. "I didn't mean to do that," she whispered. "You surprised me."

She glanced at him from the corners of her eyes. The white shirt he wore contrasted sharply with his sun-bronzed skin. If it hadn't been for the green eyes and the careless ease of his posture, he might have been taken for a Spaniard.

When he pushed the stained Stetson farther back on his head, Leah met his eyes, her brow creasing in worry. "You shouldn't be here. Pa gave orders to the men to run you off the minute you set foot on Bar R land." She paused, frowning. "What a stupid name for a ranch. Have you ever realized how hard that is to say?" She shook her head in exasperation at her wandering thoughts.

His strong lips curved upward in a slow smile. "When you shake your head like that, your hair catches little pieces of the sun and holds them right to it."

"Did you hear me?" she asked, wanting to shake him for being so stubborn. "You have to leave before any of the men come along. There'd be trouble sure as the world if one of them saw you talking to me."

"The only trouble I'm likely to have is keepin' my eyes off you. You look real nice in that blue dress." He stooped to pick a yellow daisy. "This little flower is as beautiful a thing as God ever made, but put it next to you and it winces in shame." He gently tucked the flower behind her ear.

The intensity in his eyes as he gazed down at her brought a warm, shivery sensation to her middle. "I like daisies," she murmured. "I like to see them growing out here, so wild and free." She drew a long breath, trying to slow her racing heartbeat. "I like them even better than the pink roses that grow on the side of the preacher's house." She frowned. "Besides, I think roses make me sneeze."

He chuckled and the deep, rich sound brought her gaze back to his face. "I missed you, but—"

"I missed you, too," he said quietly, his expression almost stern. "It was only two days, but it felt like a month in hell. You're doin' something to me, Leah. Something I didn't expect. All those years when I was in prison, I thought all I wanted was to get out of there and get my land back. I figure that's what kept me alive. Now"—his hand shook slightly as he reached out to touch her face—"the land doesn't matter. Nothin' matters. You're all I can think about."

Her pulse throbbed wildly in her temple where his fingers had been. Listening to him talk was like having heaven come down and wrap itself around her. It was so sweet, she was afraid suddenly. Afraid that something would happen and she would never feel this way again.

Moistening her lips, she took a step backward. "You've got to leave," she whispered. "There will be trouble, and I don't think I could stand that. Pa is so stubborn. I can't even talk to him about you. You know how he—"

She broke off, a frown tugging at her lips, confusion filling her brown yes. "Paul," she said abruptly, "is this another dream?"

He shrugged. "I reckon so, ma'am, else I wouldn't be talkin' in this damn fool way."

Her eyes sparkled as soft laughter welled up in her throat, but the sound faded away when he reached out to brush a strand of hair from her face. "I—I really think you'd better leave now."

"I'll leave." His gaze slid over her face, lingering on her lips. "But first . . ."

With movements designed to cause her no alarm, he slowly tilted her chin and lowered his mouth to hers. She drew in a sharp breath, but it was his breath she drew in. His lips moved softly across hers, holding her mesmerized with the pure pleasure they brought.

Leah had never been kissed before. Not by a man who was kissing her as a woman. No one had told her that such a simple touch could be so beautiful. No one had told her it would be so achingly sweet that she would rather die than let it go.

Throughout the kiss, her arms remained limply at her sides, and when he finally drew away, with movements as slow and cautious as his approach, she hadn't moved the whole time. But inside, she had flown. And inside, she felt that he was tearing away a piece of her when he withdrew.

For a moment he stared down at her; then he turned and walked back to the patiently waiting sorrel. Long after he and the horse had disappeared over the top of the hill, Leah stood where Paul had left her. Then, slowly, she walked back to her flowers, picked them up, and headed toward the house.

Leah wiped her hands on her apron, then took it off and hung it on a hook by the door. She had finished the dishes and knew she should go back in and join her father and their two guests, but still she hung back.

Because Slim was the Bar R's foreman, he really didn't count as a guest. And because Leah liked him, he wasn't the reason for her reluctance to rejoin the men. It was the other guest that kept her in the kitchen. She didn't like Trent Howard, and she couldn't understand why he had been spending so much time here lately. Why was he wasting his time on a barely scraping-along rancher like her father?

Trent's spread was one of the largest in the territory, which made him one of the area's most influential men. That was how men were judged in these parts. It didn't matter how good a man was, or how wise, or even how much money he had in the bank. The thing that made him important was how long it took to ride around his spread.

Leah's father's land was a dogtrot compared to Trent Howard's, but that didn't make it less important to Bob French. He was the same as all men. The land came first and everything else a poor second.

In the six years since her mother's death there had been too many times when Leah had ached to let her anger out. She had wanted to scream at her father and ask him why he couldn't have given her mother some of the love, some of the care, he gave to his precious land. But she knew she would never do it. A woman couldn't buck reality. And the reality was that in this part of the country, land was everything. Men killed and cheated and died for it. It was the wife who shared their dreams; it was the child they worried over; it was the mistress they lusted after. It was the god they worshiped.

For just a little while, if it was spring and if a man was sensitive, like Paul, he might think something—a woman, perhaps—was more important than the land. But that feeling didn't last long. Leah knew it and accepted it and resented it with all her heart.

Inhaling, she put a pleasant expression on her face and walked back into the front room. The three men still sat at the wooden table. Her father had brought out glasses and a bottle of whiskey.

"You sure outdid yourself tonight, Miss Leah," the short stocky foreman said.

"Thank you, Slim," she said, smiling. "I'll pretend you don't say that even when I burn the beans or leave the salt out of the stew."

"No, Slim's right," Trent Howard said, smiling.

His gaze ran over her body in a way that was so obvious, it made her clench her fists. She studied the man who had made her uneasy from the first moment they met. There was nothing on the surface that she could criticize. His blond hair and mustache were neatly trimmed, giving his handsome face an authoritative, moneyed look. The dark suit that fitted his frame like a glove was the best that could be had in this part of the world. No, she decided, there was nothing on the surface to cause complaint. It was the inner man that she despised and feared.

"You're a wonderful cook, my dear," Trent continued, leaning back casually in the worn wooden chair. "It's just a shame a beautiful woman like you has to spend all her time cooking and cleaning."

"I like it," she said. Although she had tried, she hadn't been able to keep a touch of belligerence out of her voice. Shifting her gaze to her father, she raised one slender eyebrow. "Well, Pa? I haven't heard from you yet. Do you think I'm wasted in the kitchen?"

His eyes didn't quite meet hers, and his smile was nervous. "You know I like your cookin', Leah, honey. But that don't keep me from wishin' you had some help around here. Too much work makes a woman old before her time."

Like Mama, she thought, feeling the pulse throb in her temple. She only wished she could believe that her father regretted all he had put her mother through. But Leah knew better. She also knew that it wasn't hard work that had made her mother grow old too soon. It was a hard man that had done that, the hard man she had married.

"If you're worried about me working too hard, Slim could always take over the washing," she said, smiling at the foreman. "What do you think, Slim? Do you want me to tell you how much starch Pa likes in his Sunday shirts?"

Slim grinned at her. "I think chasin' loco steers don't sound too bad right now."

Leah's father cleared his throat, and Leah intercepted the silent message he sent to his foreman. It told him clearly to shut up for a while.

Leah frowned, wondering what her father was plotting. His tanned, leathery features contained too much innocence. He was up to something that he wasn't sure Leah would like.

Trent Howard stood and smiled at Leah. "After that fine meal, I think I need to stretch my legs. Would you care to take a walk with me, Leah?"

Even as an excuse was forming in her thoughts, her father said, "Now there's a fine idea. Just what you need, honey—some fresh air. No, don't say a word. Fact is, there's something I need to talk to Slim about, and it would be boring for you two young people."

Young people? she thought dryly as she was ushered out the door by her father. Trent Howard had to be forty if he was a day.

The moon lighted their path as they walked across the small, bare yard toward the corral. When they reached it, Trent leaned against the wooden rail and stared down at her.

"There's a real peaceful feel to being around you, Leah," he said gently. "I like that in a woman. As a matter of fact, you're everything I like in a woman."

"That's very kind of you, Mr. Howard," she murmured, feeling uncomfortable under his intense gaze.

He smiled and shook his head. "Don't you think we've been friends long enough for you to call me Trent?"

They had never been friends and never would be, but Leah didn't argue. "Trent," she said politely.

"Sounds good when you say it. You're the quiet kind of woman that makes a man want to say things he wouldn't normally say." Sadness flitted across his handsome, dishonest features. "I've been a widower for a long time now, Leah. After a while, a man gets lonely for female companionship."

Leah kept her expression blank. She didn't remind him that he had been a widower for exactly three months. Or that, according to gossip, several females in town had had his constant companionship both before and after his wife died.

Those were things she wanted to say. What she actually said was, "We all miss your dear wife...Trent."

"Yes," he said irritably, as though it was plain bad manners for her to have mentioned his late wife. Then, like a snake shedding a useless skin, he shrugged off the mood and picked up her hand.

"Leah," he said firmly, "I'm a man who likes to put all his cards on the table. I've got a lot to give a woman. But then, I don't suppose I have to tell you that. The name Trent Howard means something in this territory. A wife of mine would never want for anything."

Except maybe a little tenderness and humanity in her husband, Leah thought, feeling anger well up inside her. How well she remembered the nervous, frightened face of the late Mrs. Howard. And even a man with Trent's power couldn't completely quell the rumors about Sarah Howard. Rumors that said her death had not been an accident, as Trent and his handpicked officials had claimed.

And now, she thought tightly, apparently with her father's blessing, this mean, cold-blooded man had decided Leah would do for his next marital victim.

When she didn't respond, Trent frowned. "There are plenty of women in the territory who would jump at the chance of being my wife. But I don't want any of them, Leah. Since the first time I saw you, I knew you would be the next Mrs. Trent Howard."

"Really?" she said, glancing away from him. "Since we met four years ago, it seems a little strange that you were thinking about your second wife before you'd gotten rid—that is, while you were still married to your first."

He sighed heavily. "Sarah was never the woman for me. Our marriage was a mistake. I didn't realize how big a mistake until I met you. Of course, I had no hope that you would actually be mine. If that tragic accident hadn't taken Sarah from me, I would still be her faithful, devoted husband. But even that wouldn't have stopped me from thinking about you." He smiled, tightening his fingers on her hand. "Don't you know what I'm saying? I'm asking you to be my wife."

He waited in expectant silence. Leah pulled her hand out of his, slowly wiping it on her skirt as she met his eyes. "No, thank you."

It was a moment before he took in what she had said; then surprise and anger flared in his brown eyes. "What do you mean, 'No, thank you'?"

"I mean I am aware of the great honor you do me in asking me to be your wife, but I must decline."

His eyes narrowed, as though he were working out a puzzle. Then he stood up straighter, in a deliberately intimidating movement. "Your womanly modesty becomes you, my dear, but I'm not a man for games." The words were clipped and hard. "I will arrange the wedding for next week—now go in and tell your father the good news."

"I also dislike games," she said calmly. "There's no need to tell Pa anything, because there will be no wedding."

His face reddened in rage. "You force me to be blunt. With or without your consent, you'll marry me."

She studied his features. "Blunt? Very well, let's be blunt. I wouldn't have you if you came postage paid and gift wrapped in shiny paper. I don't love you—I don't even like you. I believe you either killed your wife or made her so miserable that she took her own life just to get some peace. I believe you are solely responsible for Paul going to prison for a robbery he didn't commit just so you'd get your hands on his ranch." She paused, inhaling deeply. "Marry you?" she said, her voice filled with contempt. "I'd rather lie down with a rattlesnake."

"You bitch," he ground out, grasping her upper arm with cruel fingers. "By God, you'll pay for that once we're married. And what's all this about Paul Gregory? Have you been seeing him?"

Leah bit her lip. "This has nothing to do with Paul," she said nervously. "I'm simply trying to make you understand that I could never respect a man of your character."

"I don't give a damn for your respect. And you will marry me." Suddenly a strange, smug look came into his eyes and he was calm again, but when he smiled he was no longer pretending to be pleasant. "Before you say any more, you'd better go inside and talk to your father."

"What does my father have to do with this?" Her mouth had gone dry. He was too confident. What had Pa done now?

"Your father has had several bad years," Trent said, still smiling. "He would have gone under if I hadn't loaned him the money to get back on his feet again." He paused, watching her closely as he drew out the tension. "I can call in that loan any time I damn well please."

"You're lying," she whispered. "He wouldn't have done anything so stupid."

"You think not? Go ask him."

Whirling around, she ran back to the house. She shoved open the door and stood there, her breathing erratic. The two men at the table looked at her in surprise.

Without preamble, she said, "Did you borrow money from Trent Howard?"

Her father looked startled; then he glanced away, avoiding her eyes. "What kind of bee do you have in your bonnet now?'' he grumbled. ''You wear a man out—always takin' off in fits and starts.''

''Answer me, damn you!''

He stood up abruptly, knocking the chair over in the process. ''Don't you talk to me like that, missy. I'm still your pa. What I do with Bar R is my business.'' He shifted uncomfortably under her accusatory stare. ''Trent Howard saved my neck—and yours, too, if you want to know the truth of it.''

''And now I'm supposed to marry a man I don't love just because you've been stupid?'' she asked incredulously.

''Hold on, now.'' He took a step toward her, while Slim shrank back in his chair, as though trying to disappear. ''It's time you had a family of your own,'' her father said coaxingly. ''There ain't no better catch in the territory than Trent Howard. You oughtta be proud that he picked you.''

His smile died, and perspiration sprang out on his forehead as he studied the stubborn set of her chin. Raking a hand through his thin hair, he said, ''Leah, honey, you got to marry him. You got to do it, or I'll lose everything.''

She held on to the door handle to keep from swaying. ''What kind of father are you?'' she whispered hoarsely. ''How could you try to force your own flesh and blood into such an abominable agreement? It's cruel. It's selfish.'' Standing up straighter, she frowned at the two men. ''Besides, it's so trite.''

''Beg pardon?'' her father said, watching her warily, as though she had finally gone off the deep end.

She sighed and began to pace back and forth in the small room. "Unless I marry Trent, he'll call in the loan and we'll lose the ranch," she said. "It's so . . . so unimaginative. You might as well have lost me in a poker game."

"Miss Leah!" Slim's voice was shocked. "You know your pa don't gamble."

"Oh, never mind," she muttered irritably. After a moment she turned her head and met her father's gaze squarely. "You're an old fool," she said.

For a moment she felt worn down by sadness. Her father had never really loved her. When it came to a choice between her and the land, he hadn't even hesitated. His daughter was nothing more than expendable goods, a down payment on the only thing he really loved.

Turning away from the sight of her father, she saw Trent standing in the doorway, his features smooth with satisfaction. "Are you ready to talk now?" he asked politely.

She passed him without a word and walked back toward the corral. She had taken only a few steps when he caught her by the arm and swung her violently around to face him.

"Let's get something straight right now. I don't stand for temper in my women." He pushed his hand beneath her hair, grasping her neck with hurtful fingers. "Now's as good a time as any for me to show you who's boss."

"Don't be stupid," she said sharply. "Pa might want me to marry you, but he won't stand by and see me abused."

"Your father will do whatever I want him to," he said, his iron fingers pulling her closer.

"No!" She pushed at his chest with all her strength, but her struggles were useless. Dragging breath into her lungs, she screamed, and the sound rose around them, piercing the air. Then, abruptly, her desperate cry was smothered by his mouth.

She hated it. It was wrong, so wrong. It wasn't a kiss; it was a physical intrusion on her rights as a human being. This act of violence was a world away from the gentle, loving caress she had received from Paul. The tender flesh of her lips was ground cruelly against her clenched teeth. When she felt his tongue probing, violating her, an uncontrollable shudder of revulsion racked her limbs. He dug his fingers deeply into her neck, but still she refused to unclench her teeth. Though panic numbed her mind, she knew she had to fight him, even if he beat her senseless.

"You stubborn bitch," he rasped out. Twisting his fingers in her hair, he jerked viciously. "Open your mouth."

I won't faint, she told herself. I won't let him see weakness in me.

Unclenching her teeth, she allowed him to push his tongue in slightly, then she bit him. He swore, shoving her away with enough force to make her stumble. Breathing harshly, Leah began to back away from the look in his eyes.

He's going to murder me, she thought. He's going to kill me like he killed Sarah.

She saw her father and Slim on the porch, but now Leah knew there would be no help from them. Pa would see her raped in his yard if it meant he could save his land, and Slim would do whatever her father told him to do. An instant of despair weakened her; then she raised her chin, her eyes flaring. Whatever happened, she would not allow her weakness to aid Trent Howard's victory.

Suddenly Leah stiffened and raised her head to listen. The sound she had thought was the pounding of her own heart was growing louder. And now she recognized it for what it was—hoofbeats. Someone was riding hard and fast. And he was coming toward the ranch.

A moment later she could see the horse in the moonlight, coming straight at her and the man beside her. A muffled sound came from Trent seconds before he jumped out of the way. But Leah stood her ground. It could be only one person, and that person brought her no fear.

Paul reined in fiercely, causing his horse to rear in protest. He reached down to grab Leah under her arms, and she was plucked off the ground. As he swung her around, she dragged up her skirt and flung herself astride the saddle, close behind him. Then, before Trent even had a chance to move, Paul dug his spurs into the horse's flanks, and they galloped away into the enveloping darkness, leaving the three men on the ground to watch in helpless fury.

Leah gripped Paul's waist tightly, pressing her face into his back. He didn't slow the furious pace, even when they left her father's land, and so speech between them was impossible. Then, when the terrain became rougher, he allowed the horse to pick its way through the rocks.

Even then Leah didn't question him. It was enough that he had come for her.

Several hours after they had left the ranch it began to rain. Not a gentle spring shower, but hard, steady sheets of icy rain. And still they didn't stop. Several times the horse lost its footing, slithering sideways in the slick mud. But each time Paul's body seemed to turn to iron under her hands, and as if by sheer force of will, he would right the stumbling beast and they would keep going.

By the time the movement beneath her stopped, Leah was in a state of exhausted semi-awareness. Paul jumped down, catching her in his arms as she slid sideways in the saddle.

He carried her into a small cabin and stood her on her feet just inside the door, leaving her to light a lantern that sat in the middle of a rough wooden table. Within seconds he was back, holding a dark blanket.

"You need to get out of those wet clothes," he said, handing her the blanket. Then he turned his back to her and squatted in front of a small stone fireplace.

The blanket slid through her numb fingers. She left it on the floor and began to fumble with the hooks and eyes that ran down the front of her dress. The wet fabric clung to her body and seemed to fight her efforts, but eventually she stepped out of it and removed her undergarments.

She wrapped the blanket around her, clutching it tightly as she tried to keep her teeth from chattering. "I'm through." Her voice was a weak thread that barely penetrated the silence.

He stood immediately and turned to face her, moving her toward the fire with a hand on her waist. "You sit here and get warm." Without another word, he walked to the door and opened it.

"Paul! Where are you going?" The panic in the words shamed her, and she glanced away from his searching gaze.

"I've got to see to my horse," he said quietly. "It won't take long."

She nodded; then, when she heard the door close, she slumped to the floor, wrapping her arms around her blanket-covered knees.

Was he angry with her? she wondered, blinking back the tears that stung her eyes. The gentle, laughing man she had seen earlier today was gone and a solemn stranger had taken his place. Did Paul resent her for bringing this trouble down on him?

Gradually the warmth from the fire began to reach her, and the tremors that shook her body died away. She fell into a state of mental and emotional numbness as she stared into the leaping, crackling flames.

When the door to the cabin opened once again, she didn't look up but kept her gaze straight ahead. She could hear him moving around the cabin; then, minutes later, he sat beside her before the fire.

Finally Leah turned her face toward him. He had removed his wet shirt, exposing the muscles of his shoulders and arms. A sprinkling of dark hair spread across his chest, narrowing to a V that trailed down his hard, flat stomach, then disappeared at the waist of his still-damp pants.

Jerking her gaze upward, she found him staring at her face, a frown adding harsh lines to his tanned features.

"You don't have to be afraid, Leah," he said. "I won't ever let him touch you again."

She shook her head. "I'm not afraid of Trent. Not now. It's just—" She broke off, biting her lip. "Are you angry with me, Paul?" She couldn't keep a slight tremor from her voice.

He inhaled sharply. "Never," he said with deep intensity. "I didn't mean to give that impression. I'm worried about you, Leah. I didn't give you a chance to think about this." He took both her hands in his, his expression somber as he searched her face. "Trent Howard wants you. Although he'd rather see you dead than with me, he knows it wouldn't be necessary to kill you. I couldn't watch over you every minute of the day. He has too many men and too much influence here. Sooner or later he'd kill me, and then there would be no one to keep you safe." His fingers tightened on hers. "You know what that means, don't you? It means we can't stay here. Leah, if you come with me, you won't ever see your father again."

His features softened, and when he spoke again the words were so filled with tenderness that it felt as if someone was squeezing her heart. "I made my decision the minute I heard you scream. Now you have to make yours. If you want, I can take you back as soon as it stops raining."

She kept her eyes trained on his face. "Don't you know?" she whispered. "There's no decision to make. As long as I'm with you, nothing else, no one else in the world, matters."

Joy so great that it left her weak exploded in his green eyes as he crushed her to his chest. A violent tremor shook his strong body, and now Leah recognized the tight control he had held on his emotions as he gave her a choice.

Moments later, he framed her face with rough hands. "We'll have a good life, Leah. There won't be much at first, but for the rest of my life, you'll be loved so damned hard, it'll make you dizzy." She laughed, feeling the dizziness already. "And someday," he continued, "I'll come back here. I'll come back, and I'll set things right with Trent Howard."

Leah felt herself stiffen. After a moment she nodded sadly and pulled away from him, gazing into the fire. Always the land, she thought wearily. But he was her man now. She would take that part of him along with the rest. Because without Paul there was nothing.

"I understand what the land means to you, Paul," she said slowly. "Are—are you sure you wouldn't rather stay and fight it out now? You wouldn't have to worry about me. I could go somewhere else for a while. I—"

"Leah!" He grasped her shoulders tightly, turning her to face him. "What are you talking about?" He examined her face, frowning at the pain he found in her eyes. "What's hurting you?" he asked in bewilderment. "Why are you talking about my land? It's not for the land that I'll settle with Trent Howard. Sure, every man wants a place of his own, somewhere he can put down roots. But my roots aren't tied up in a piece of ground. My roots are wherever you are. When I come back here, it'll just be to set things right. If I let Howard get away with what he's done to *both* of us, I would be a poor sort of man. And you deserve more than that, Leah."

As he spoke, Leah felt a great yearning and softening within her, a sweet warmth even more powerful than what she had felt when he kissed her in the field. The bonds that had held her prisoner loosened, then fell away completely. He really meant it. She was more important to him than the land. She was as important to him as he was to her.

Paul kept his eyes on her face, and he must have seen the happiness that had become a steady glow, because a smile spread across his face.

"Where will we go?" she said, the weariness in her voice replaced by shy enthusiasm. It didn't matter where they went. They could go to the moon for all she cared, as long as they were together. She just wanted to hear the sound of his voice.

"Well," he said lazily, his eyes crinkling with amusement, "have you ever thought about Texas?"

She shook her head. "No. Is it nice?"

He laughed. "That's a pretty tame word for Texas. It's not like here. It's wild and free, and there's plenty of good land for cattle."

She loved hearing the excitement in his voice. She didn't even care that he mentioned land. He could have a million acres now and it wouldn't bother her. "It sounds wonderful," she said earnestly.

"I hope you still think so when you see it. It's big, Leah. So big, it'll make your head swim. It can be green and gentle, or it can be dry and hellishly hot."

She touched his face. "It sounds to me as if you even like the hellish part."

"I do," he admitted, grinning. "There's a place in the western part I want to show you. We couldn't live there—it's too wild and mean even for cattle, but it's beautiful. Maybe someday I can take you there just to see it." His gaze was steady, as though he were seeing his wild Texas country now. "You can stand on the side of a mountain I know of and look out over hundreds of miles of country.... The color of it will make you drunk. It's like looking at the day the earth was born. It has the feel of forever to it."

He came back from Texas and was now looking only at Leah, his features softened with love. "When you look at me, your eyes turn golden with sparks of bronze fire in them. They remind me of sunset on those rocks. It's as if God took melted gold and splashed it on everything. I want to show you that, Leah. I want to show you what it feels like when I look in your eyes."

She couldn't take her gaze from his face. He was so beautiful. She didn't need his west Texas mountain to know what forever looked like. It looked like green eyes and a fiercely loving heart.

He raised a hand and ran the tips of his fingers down her throat and over her shoulder, pushing the blanket away with the same light, compelling stroke. Fiery threads of desire tightened in her, making her tremble beneath his touch, and with a simple shrug of her shoulders, the blanket fell and settled around her hips.

The breath caught roughly in his throat. He closed his eyes, his head thrown back as the muscles of his tanned face tautened, giving him the look of carved teak. The fingers on her shoulder tightened painfully, but she welcomed the pain. In some way it seemed to make her a part of him.

Slowly he opened his eyes. "You're not fighting it anymore—this thing between us." It wasn't a question. It was a statement filled with wonder.

On a distant level, she knew he was talking about a reality beyond the cabin, beyond this place and time.

"No," she whispered. "I'm not fighting it."

He groaned her name, pushing her to the floor as he kissed her with a possessiveness that made her weak. His tongue slid between her lips, branding her, making her his own. Her breasts pushed against the wonderful roughness of his bare chest, bringing a sweet and terrible ache to her body.

His hand began to move urgently on her flesh, down her back and the gentle curve of her hip, lingering on her birthmark. Raising his head, he buried his face in her hair.

"I've been so lonely." The roughly whispered words were filled with remembered pain. "I thought I could do without you, love, without your warmth. But now I know I was only fooling myself. All my life, something's been missing, but until I held you the first time, I didn't even know what it was. I only knew there was an unexplainable emptiness in me, as if my soul was a house where no one lived anymore."

Wrapping her arms around him, she held him tightly, wanting to share the hurt, needing to fill the emptiness. His hard, smooth flesh rippled beneath her fingers, and he arched against her uncontrollably, making her feel his urgent need, bringing a fever to her blood.

Then he moved away from her slightly and brought a strong, tanned hand to her breast. The tips of his fingers brushed across the dusky nipple, and it sprang to life beneath his touch. Slowly, he bent and took the taut bud between his teeth, making her gasp with pleasure. Looking down, she saw him suck it deep into his mouth. With desperate fingers she held him to her, feeling the heat spread through her with the speed and power of lightning.

When his hand slid to her inner thigh, she moved against it, wanting to capture the wildness and beauty of the sensations he was offering with every caress.

A tiny whimpering sound escaped her when he stood abruptly. Her eyes were glazed with deep hunger as she watched him remove the rest of his clothes.

There was no shyness in her now. This man belonged to her. She stared openly, watching as the firelight flickered across the strong body before her. She felt a tightness grow in her chest and an unbearable ache grow in her loins.

He shuddered under her gaze for a second before he rejoined her on the blanket. Running a hand down the length of her body, he united their flesh, pressing her breasts to his chest, her stomach to his hard belly, her restless hips to his burning need.

Instinctively, his lips sought hers, making her feel the fiery hunger in him. And when his hand slipped between her thighs, she opened herself to him with a desire that matched his own.

"Now, love," he whispered, his voice harsh.

When he moved over her, Leah felt her muscles tighten in anticipation. "Yes—now," she moaned urgently. "Now, Paul."

She was dying for him. Her trembling fingers pressed his hard, lean hips, telling him as much as her words, urging him to her. Any second now she would know the joy that she had been waiting all her life to find. Any second . . .

* * *

"No—*not now!*" Leah gasped. "I can't wake up *now!*"

The furious words startled her into full awareness, and her gaze darted frantically around her dark bedroom. Her skin was slick with perspiration. Her body burned and ached with a depth that shook her. The covers were twisted around her as she lay still, willing her heart to stop pounding in her chest.

She held her clenched fists at her sides, trying to keep from screaming in frustration. For a long time she merely lay there with her eyes wide open; then, with a hoarse groan, she rolled over and buried her face in the pillow, knowing there would be no more sleep for her the rest of the night.

Chapter Five

You draw me, you hard-hearted adamant;

A Midsummer Night's Dream—Act II, Scene 2

Leah sat in the armchair across the room from her bed, her arms wrapped around her legs, her chin resting on her knees. For the first time in four years she didn't want to go to work. She wanted to call in sick. The only thing that stopped her was her meeting this morning with Paul to go over the differences in the two campaigns.

Paul. Yes, she thought of him as Paul now. How could she not? She had tried so many times to convince herself that her superior was not the man in her dreams, but it was beginning to be impossible. God, she moaned silently, the whole thing was impossible.

Every time she closed her eyes she saw him in the cabin, the firelight leaping across the hard, lean lines of his bronzed body, and her stomach muscles would constrict in immediate involuntary reaction.

I don't want this, she thought in desperation. She didn't want a man with her boss's face to be tender and loving. She didn't want to remember the loneliness and painfully deep need that had shone out of his green eyes. And she couldn't handle the fierce sensuality in him that sent desire ripping through her body every time she thought of it.

Where was her famous objectivity now? she asked herself with a twisted smile. Where was her much-admired logic?

"Gone up in dreams," she murmured, then pressed her face to her knees with a groan.

Think about them, she told herself. Don't let them control you. Take them apart and show yourself there's nothing of substance there. It's all airy-fairy stuff. Night visions. Wispy pieces of unreality.

Inhaling slowly, she raised her head. There had been three dreams. Good start, she thought with heavy sarcasm. Three dreams. Then what?

The dreams were hokey, but if she overlooked the bad scripts and concentrated on the two main characters—Paul and herself—what were the dreams telling her?

Each dream seemed to point out different nuances of Paul's personality. They had shown her things about him that had surprised her because of her admittedly prejudiced view of him. She had seen his humor and spirit in the Roman dream, his fire and sensuality in the twenties dream, his tenderness and vulnerability in the Western dream.

Why? she asked herself, her brow creasing with the depths of her concentration. Why had she been shown these things?

Leah shook her head helplessly. She simply didn't know. To make it even more confusing, reality had begun to reinforce what she had seen in the dreams. She had seen his humor the night they had dinner together. She had seen his tenderness when he talked to the little boy on the escalator.

And his fire? His sensuality?

Moaning, she buried her face in her knees again. Please—no, she thought in desperation. She definitely didn't want to see the sensuality. Enough was enough.

Stop it, you idiot, she told herself sternly. *Think!*

Leaning her head back against the chair, she rubbed her chin thoughtfully with her knuckles. Could it be that she had subconsciously picked up on facets of Paul's personality without being aware of it? Maybe she was merely playing back the hidden information in her dreams.

She shifted restlessly. That was a definite possibility. But why now? And why were the dreams showing her things about herself that were totally opposed to reality?

Or were they simply opposed to her idea of reality? she wondered in confusion. Reluctantly she admitted that the original attraction she had felt for Paul was

still there, and just as strong as ever. The crazy dreams
had forced her to face up to that. But sacrificing her
security and even her life for love? Was the potential
for that kind of thing really buried somewhere in her
subconscious?

And again, why now? she asked herself stubbornly. And why did the dreams take such a peculiar
form? They all had seemed like silly little fragments
from old, low-budget movies.

She sat up straighter. Movies? she thought, frowning.

Her feet slid to the floor, and there was a stunned
look on her face as she absently pushed the hair from
her forehead. *Movies.* Each of the dreams had come
on a night when she had worked late. And every time
she had worked late she had—

Jumping from the chair, she ran to the living room
and jerked open the cabinet that held the videotapes.
She ran a finger over the small stack that she had already played, working from the bottom up. *For Cae-
sar We Die...G-Men: The Chicago Story...Cattle
Country.*

For a long time Leah simply stood staring at them.
Then she began to laugh. She laughed so hard that she
slumped to the floor in front of the cabinet to keep
from falling. Tears streamed down her face, and every
time she tried to pull herself together, she would glance
at the tapes, and the whole thing would start over
again.

All that intense soul-searching for naught, she
thought, shaking her head helplessly. She had been

trying to find some deep, psychological meaning in the dreams, when all along they had been nothing more than a combination of overwork, an understandable but hidden attraction to Paul, and the old movies she always played while she worked.

Drawing in a shaky breath, she rose to her feet and closed the cabinet doors. When she recognized just how overwhelming her relief was, Leah knew how much those dreams had been worrying her.

"From now on," she murmured ruefully, "I'll listen to the radio when I work late."

In the next few months Leah listened to the radio a lot. As she had expected, there were no more dreams, but she barely had time to notice. The candidates for the San Francisco job had been narrowed down to three, and she was still in the running. She had the advantage of being in the home office, while the other two had to be flown in for interviews.

And always, there was the new ad campaign. Work on the project was in full swing now, which meant that she and Paul spent more time together than ever before. He had unbent so far as to occasionally call her Leah, but even though she thought of him as Paul, she was careful never to say the name aloud. Now that she had finally gotten control of her subconscious, she didn't want anything rocking the boat.

At her suggestion, Paul had decided to use Universal personnel in the campaign rather than hire an actor or sports figure as spokesperson. It wouldn't be the Fly Me type of thing that showed cute, young flight attendants flirting with the camera. They would use mechanics, food-service people, ticket-counter personnel—everyone who made Universal the airline it was.

To her surprise, Paul had put Leah in charge of finding just the right people for the commercials. It wasn't a surprise, however, to find that she loved being in charge. Promising candidates were flown in from all over the world so that she could interview them. Out of hundreds, she and Paul had chosen the brightest, the most enthusiastic, the most photogenic.

Then, one evening in early fall, it all came together. All the people involved in the new campaign—people from both Universal and the advertising agency—gathered together in one of Universal's largest conference rooms.

The room was packed tight with people, all waiting anxiously for the same thing. The newspaper ads had come out that morning, and the radio spots had run several times during the day. Now they were gathered for the most important part—the airing of the first television commercial.

Leah had seen it before, but test runs at the ad agency weren't the same as the real thing. She could never really judge the quality of a commercial until she knew that millions of other people were watching it at the same time. For some reason, then she could see it through their eyes.

"Quiet!" someone shouted. "Everbody shut up. Ten seconds until it airs."

The low rumble in the room died instantly, and Leah turned with everyone else to watch the television mounted high on the wall at the end of the conference table. She saw Paul standing on the other side of the room and took a moment to wonder if he felt as nervous as she did. When their eyes met for an instant, she could detect nothing vulnerable in his stern features. Slowly, he raised a dark eyebrow, and somehow it almost seemed a sign of encouragement.

Turning back to the television, Leah felt every muscle tense as the situation comedy faded to black for a commercial break. Then, as the screen brightened with a vivid scene, she relaxed, and a smile of pure joy dissolved the tension in her features.

Three seconds into the commercial, she knew it was exactly right. It was a quality piece, the tone perfect—it wasn't glamorous, but neither was it ordinary. It sparkled with vitality and excitement. Without actually saying the words, it used bright shots and enthusiastic people to say, "Life is made to enjoy—let Universal Air show you how."

When the commercial faded, the silence exploded with the sound of applause and popping champagne corks. Relief and exhilaration spread across the room in an almost visible wave. People began moving—laughing, patting themselves and others on the back, grabbing glasses filled with sparkling wine. Over and over again they repeated to each other that they had known all along it would be a success.

Leah soon found herself surrounded by a swarm of people, all offering congratulations. More than once she heard herself called a genius, and a couple of times the praise even sounded sincere. If she hadn't possessed such a stable personality, she might have had trouble keeping her head from floating skyward. But she had been in the business long enough to know that within a week she would be just another advertising executive.

Later, when the noise had built to a deafening level, Charlotte came to stand beside Leah. Or, rather, she came to hide behind her. As shy as she was in the office, it was no wonder that Charlotte was intimidated by the rowdy crowd.

"Have some champagne, Charlotte," Leah urged, reaching behind her to grab a bottle and refill Charlotte's glass. "Loosen up a little."

Charlotte made a face and swallowed a big gulp of the wine. "Are they always so wild?" she asked, her blue eyes darting nervously around the room.

Leah grinned. She had forgotten that this was her secretary's first campaign. "You think this is wild?" Leah said. "Wait a couple of hours until they have a few gallons of champagne under their belts. That's when Leonard Posner takes off his clothes and does the Hustle on the conference table."

Charlotte's plain features paled slightly, but behind her glasses, the blue eyes were just a little intrigued. "Really?" she whispered.

Leah put an arm around the other woman to give her a laughing hug. "You silly baby," she said. "Leonard is most likely hiding in the hall, like he does every year. No one gets more than a little high at these things—or, if they do, it's on excitement, not the champagne. Relax and have a good time . . . but don't let anyone pull you into a closet, and take any vows of undying love with a grain of salt. No one will remember a word they've said tomorrow.''

"Not only beautiful—brilliant as well.''

Both women turned to find Lester Walker standing on the other side of Leah.

"Hello, Les.'' Leah smiled stiffly at the stocky blond man. She hadn't forgotten the scene in his office, but apparently he had. Or maybe he thought she wouldn't embarrass him in public. It wouldn't be the first time Lester had been mistaken about her.

"I take it you liked the commercial,'' she said, her expression indifferent.

"As I said—brilliant.'' He raised his champagne glass in a smiling salute. "There were a couple of minor things I might have changed, but, on the whole, it was brilliant. I can't help wondering what it would have been like if we had combined our talents—brilliance added to brilliance, so to speak.'' He lowered his gaze to the bare flesh that showed above the white camisole Leah wore under her pale blue silk jacket. "You might keep it in mind for next time.''

Leah sighed with exaggerated weariness. "You've been thinking again, Lester,'' she said regretfully. "You know that always gives you a headache. Oh, look.'' She gestured with her glass toward the other side of the room. "That redhead from the ad agency is wiggling her hips at you. Better hurry, before she realizes she doesn't have her contacts in.''

Leah rolled her eyes as he dived into the crowd, making his way toward the unfortunate redhead.

Charlotte leaned closer to whisper, "Do you suppose he's really so...so trivial? Maybe it's just an act."

"Act my foot," Leah said, giving an unladylike snort of derision. "Scratch Lester's surface, and you'll only find more surface."

Charlotte started to giggle; then suddenly she stiffened, her gaze trained on something just beyond Leah's shoulder. An instant later, like the Cheshire cat, the brunette simply faded into the surrounding crowd.

Swinging around, Leah found Paul standing behind her. "Is Walker giving you a bad time?" he asked calmly.

"Les Walker *is* a bad time," she replied dryly; then, bracing herself, she met his eyes. "Well, what did you think?"

"It went well."

She relaxed, giving him a radiant smile. "Knowing you—and since I've had two glasses of champagne—I'll interpret that to mean it was a dazzling success." She closed her eyes briefly, drawing a deep breath. "I feel like there should be fireworks lighting up the sky, crowds throwing streamers, people dancing in the streets."

He studied her face silently, his features as composed as always. "Tomorrow you'll come down with a thud. You'll most likely wake up with a hangover due more to an excess of exhilaration than an excess of champagne."

She raised her gaze to his face, staring in curiosity. "Doesn't the excitement affect you at all, Mr. Gregory? You worked twice as hard as I did on this. Don't you feel just a little bit satisfied that it turned out so well?"

He shrugged. "It didn't turn out well by itself—we worked our butts off to make sure it turned out well. So there shouldn't be any cause for surprise that it did."

"Yes, of course," she murmured, glancing around the room for an avenue of escape. "Oh, dear, they've got poor Charlotte cornered. I'd better go rescue her."

Smiling politely, she moved away from him. She needed to be with real people right now. People who not only had emotions, but let them show. It was Leah's night and, come hell or high water, she was going to celebrate.

Two hours later Leah sat sprawled comfortably in a mahogany armchair, a half-empty glass in her hand as she stared at the stockinged but shoeless feet that were extended in front of her.

"Good night...um...oh, yeah, good night, Leah."

Leah glanced up to see Charlotte standing unsteadily beside her. Her normally meticulous secretary's brown hair was sticking out in untidy peaks all over her head, and her glasses were askew on the end of her nose.

Leah smiled and waved her hand in a lazy goodbye as the woman left the room. It was as much of an effort as she cared to make at the moment. She was by no means intoxicated, but she was very definitely, very pleasantly mellow.

The only other person in the room was Paul. He sat in a chair at the head of the conference table. But instead of his usual rigid posture, he was slumped forward across the table with an empty champagne bottle beside him.

Slowly he raised his head, resting his chin on the table, and looked at Leah. A lock of brown hair had fallen down on his forehead, and his eyes were unfocused. He blinked twice, then frowned. Leah swallowed a giggle. He was fighting so hard to look dignified.

"Miss French." The words were slightly muffled from the pressure of the table against his chin.

"Yes, sir?"

"Either you are swaying in a singularly—" he broke the word into individual syllables as he pushed himself up with his elbows "—nauseating way or..." He paused, and with an abrupt movement, dropped his head to his open palms in an effort to hold himself upright. "Or I'm sloshed," he finished, grinning broadly.

Leah couldn't hide her amusement now. She leaned back in the chair and laughed with open enjoyment. Not only was his hair disheveled, but three buttons on his shirt were undone, and the knot in his tie hung halfway down his chest. While everyone else had partied, her iron-willed boss had gotten quietly skunked.

"And since I never overindulge," he added firmly, "it must be you. Kindly cease and desist."

"Yes, sir," she murmured agreeably, then took another sip of champagne. "I'll stop swaying."

Glancing down, she carefully moved one shoe with her feet until it was directly in front of her, then began to see if she could pick it up with her toes.

She could. Smiling in satisfaction, she watched it dangle.

It was Leah's night. She could do anything. Leap tall buildings...stop speeding locomotives...pick up a shoe with her toes.

Glancing toward the table, she saw Paul rise unsteadily to his feet. "A cab," he muttered as he moved to the telephone on the cabinet behind him.

He leaned down, holding his face close to the black console as he pressed each button with great care. After a moment he broke the connection and began again. When he had repeated this process three times, Leah stood and walked across the room. She took the receiver from him and punched in the correct numbers while he peered suspiciously over her shoulder to see what magic she used to make it work.

As she gave the address to the cab company, her cool, stiff superior played with the coiled telephone wire, stretching it out, then letting it spring back, then stretching it out again.

Leah bit her lip to keep from laughing. "A cab's on the way," she said, returning the receiver to the cradle.

"Thank you very much," he said earnestly.

For a reason known only to him, he decided to bow. Leah caught him by the shoulders as he swayed forward, then pushed him back, holding him in place.

"You are excellent, Miss French," he said, the words precise and clear. "Have I ever told you how very excellent you are?"

"No, sir," she said, chuckling softly. "I don't believe you have."

"Well, you are. Excellent." He nodded emphatically. "You charm greedy businessmen. You do in two days what it would take anyone else a week to finish." He smiled. "And you dial a mean telephone."

"That's kind of you, sir, but I simply do my job."

"No," he said, shaking his head so vigorously that she had to tighten her grip on his shoulders to hold him steady. "I've been remiss in not showing my appreciation. I'll send you a dozen roses." He frowned down at her. "Make a note to remind me, Miss French."

"Yes, sir," she said solemnly as her brown eyes sparkled.

Turning away, he moved toward the table. "No, not roses. Roses make you sneeze. I'll send—" He broke off and turned the bottle upside down, then peered inside it, one eye closed tightly. "Someone's been pilfering my champagne."

"That's a shame," she said sympathetically as she removed the bottle from his hands and set it on the table. "But really, sir, you don't have time for another drink. Your cab will be here in a few minutes."

"My cab...your cab. You're right...let's go." He picked up his jacket and let her help him into it, but didn't bother to button his shirt or straighten his tie.

"I didn't celebrate quite as much as you," she said, pushing his limp arm into the correct sleeve. "I can drive my own car."

"Nonsense," he said curtly. "You'll share the cab. It's stupid to take chances."

He was definitely the vice president now, she thought ruefully. And Leah knew better than to argue with him. As they left together, she kept her eyes on him carefully, ready to catch him at any minute. But he rode the elevator down, walked across the lobby, waited for Mr. Timms to open the front door and climbed into the back seat of the cab—all with a dignity that amazed her.

Then, the minute the cab pulled away from the curb, he slid bonelessly down in the seat and closed his eyes. When Leah leaned toward him in concern, he opened his eyes and grinned at her, his expression surprisingly boyish. "I did it," he said smugly.

She laughed. "I never doubted you for a minute."

"Oh, yes, you did . . . but I forgive you." His green eyes were imperious as he gazed down his nose at her. "Lesser men would have stumbled, you know."

Oh, Mr. Gregory, she thought, chuckling in delight. You're human after all.

It was a good thing she didn't have to see him like this every day. He was funny and charming and—she broke off the thought and studied his face. With his hair mussed and his features relaxed, he appeared uncharacteristically vulnerable . . . and more than a little appealing.

At that moment the cab turned a corner, catching Paul off guard, and he slid toward Leah. Reacting instinctively, she put her arms around him to hold him up.

Slowly he raised his eyes to hers. Leah drew in a sharp breath. Flashes of gold appeared in the green, reaching out to her, holding her gaze so that it was impossible for her to look away.

But she didn't want to look away. In that second the cab disappeared and they were once more lying on a blanket in front of a flickering fire. As she stared into his eyes, she felt sweet, liquid heat spread through her body, leaving in its wake a throbbing ache.

When he lowered his lips to hers, the fireworks she had wished for earlier exploded...inside her own body. There was no hesitancy in the kiss. It was eager and hungry. It was absolutely right. She parted her lips, meeting his tongue urgently, then sighed in deep pleasure, as though she had come to the end of a long search and found something she hadn't even known she was searching for.

Gripping her waist, he pulled Leah closer, fitting her body to his with strong, sure hands. Hands that seemed to claim the curves of her body as their own.

It was only when the driver cleared his throat that reality hit Leah like a glass of cold water in the face. She gasped and pulled frantically out of Paul's arms, covering her eyes with one trembling hand.

How on earth had that happened? she wondered, her thoughts whirling in confusion. My God, how had it happened?

"We're at the apartment complex, ma'am," the driver said. "You want to show me which one?"

Embarrassed heat flooded her face. "Turn right at the first side street. It's 1106," she said hoarsely, her hands shaking as she tried to straighten her jacket.

Stiffening her shoulders, she forced herself to look at Paul. He was leaning against the side of the cab, his eyes closed. As she watched, he opened them and glanced around slowly, letting his gaze settle on her.

"Miss French," he said, his voice husky. "Did I just kiss you?"

She shook her head vehemently. "No, sir." She tried desperately to keep her voice normal. "You must have imagined it."

He sighed, closing his eyes again. "Yes, that's what I thought," he murmured.

The second the cab stopped in front of her apartment, Leah opened the door and stepped out. When she heard Paul slide across the seat toward the door, she panicked.

"No—you don't need to get out with me, Mr. Gregory," she said urgently. "I'm only two steps away from my apartment. I'll see you tomorrow, sir."

She closed the door quickly, then turned and walked away. After a moment she heard the cab drive away, and she exhaled in shaky relief.

Hours later, as she sat huddled in the chair in her bedroom, Leah stared into the darkness with wide eyes. She was more shaken than she could ever remember being. Now she had seen the fire, the sensuality. She had not only seen it, she had tasted it and felt it beneath her fingers. Her body still ached in the aftermath of desire.

Paul was lucky, she told herself. He probably wouldn't remember the kiss. But Leah didn't know if she would ever be able to forget it.

She still couldn't believe it had happened. The intensity, the strength of feeling, had rocked her very foundations. She had never imagined anything like that. Even the dreams couldn't match the power of what had just occurred between them.

She clenched her fists tightly. She couldn't let this shake her. She couldn't let a simple kiss affect her so deeply.

She knew now that her panic at the thought of becoming involved with Paul wasn't simply because she was afraid an affair would distract her from her career goals. There was much, much more to it than that. What she was beginning to feel for Paul was too compelling, too overpowering, for her to deal with. She had never asked for that kind of depth, and she didn't want it. In a way she didn't fully understand, it was a threat. A threat that shook her to her very soul.

She didn't go to bed at all that night. Several times, as she sat huddled in the chair, she drifted into a light, restless sleep. But almost immediately she would awake with a strange expectancy that bewildered and, in some indefinable way, frightened her.

When she arrived at work the next day she felt oddly disassociated from her surroundings, as though she were watching everything from a distance, as though the world had fuzzy, gray edges.

"I will never drink champagne again," she muttered as she walked into Charlotte's office. Coming to an abrupt halt, she stared at her secretary.

"What on earth happened to you?" Leah asked, still staring. Charlotte's hair looked worse than it had the night before. It looked as though she had combed it with a garden rake. And her pale eyes behind the glasses were pink and puffy.

"Leah," she whispered. Her voice was filled with horror as she glanced around to make sure no doors were open. "I think I'm engaged to *Lester*."

Leah made a choking sound and grabbed Charlotte's arm, pulling the brunette into her office and closing the door behind them.

"Sit," she said firmly as she walked around to take her own chair. "Now—would you care to expand on that?"

Charlotte pulled a crumpled tissue from her pocket and blew her nose. "I just woke up this morning and there he was, right there in the bed beside me—" she didn't even pause for breath as the words came in a constant, panicky stream "—and he didn't have any clothes on and his knees are sharp and that must have been what was poking me all night, only I didn't realize it because I thought it was one of those little plastic lumps in the electric blanket and...and..."

She finally paused, gulping for air, her pink eyes wide as she raised her gaze to Leah. "Leah, I can't tell if—I mean, I don't feel like—"

"No," Leah murmured, her voice distracted, her brown eyes blank with astonishment. "With Lester you probably wouldn't—but Charlotte, even if you..." She paused and wiggled her eyebrows expressively. "Even if you did, why would you think you're engaged to the idiot?"

The brunette frowned. "I don't know. It's just that when he was eating breakfast, he patted me on the behind and said he'd been looking for a good cook and it looked as if he'd finally found one and—"

"You cooked breakfast for him?" Leah asked, her voice indignant.

"Wasn't I supposed to?"

"The man is not looking for a good cook, he's looking for a free ride! And it's not going to be you. Damn it, Charlotte, didn't I tell you not to listen to anyone last night? And it had to be Lester, of all people." She paused, frowning. "Unless you want him." She couldn't keep the distaste from her expression.

"No!" Charlotte exclaimed urgently, jumping to her feet. "What am I going to do? He said since his car was in the shop, we could go home together—he's expecting to go home with me after work!" she said, her voice rising in hysteria. "Oh, what am I going to do?"

"Calm down." Leah began to pace. After a moment she stopped and turned to Charlotte. "Okay, here's what you do. Call him—right now, as soon as you get back to your desk—and tell him what you're going to cook for dinner tonight. Then just casually mention that your parents will be there, too, because they want to meet him." Leah's smile was wicked.

"That'll scare the pants off him…or, in this case, back on him."

"Do you really think it'll work?"

"Trust me," she said, pushing the other woman out the door. "Lester will run so fast, he'll put his sharp little knees out of joint."

Charlotte nodded and moved toward her desk; then she stopped and swung back around. "Oh Lord, Leah, I forgot. I was supposed to tell you as soon as you got here that Mr. Gregory wanted to see you right away. There was some kind of foul-up in the newspaper ads."

Leah bit her lip and moved back into her office. She wasn't ready to face him yet, but, on the other hand, the longer she put it off, the longer she would have to worry.

Leah the lionhearted, she thought derisively. Fighting love dragons for Charlotte and Faith. Solving personal problems for all and sundry. And her own personal life was so tangled it would take a Los Alamos computer to unravel it.

She wasn't worried about Paul remembering what had happened the night before—he had forgotten it even before she got out of the cab. What worried her was what she would remember and what she would feel when she saw him again.

When she walked into his office, he looked up and tossed a newspaper across the desk. "Did you see this?"

It took only a glance to see he was furious. And his anger was just what she needed to keep her on an even keel. Picking up the newspaper, she ran her gaze over the print, then frowned as she spotted the Universal ad. The wrong Universal ad.

"This ad is not supposed to run until just before Christmas," she said in confusion.

"You're very quick, Miss French." His voice was heavy with sarcasm as he leaned back in the chair. "So why in hell is it running today?"

She shook her head, still frowning. "I don't know, but I'll get it straightened out."

"Yes, you will," he said emphatically. "Mr. Rose of the *Morning Star* will see you in his office at ten sharp—and he'd better give you a damn good explanation for this kind of foul-up."

"Yes, sir," she said. "I'll make sure—" She broke off, glancing at the man across the desk. "Mr. Rose?"

"Rose," he repeated impatiently. "If he ran this on orders from the ad agency, just—"

Leah missed the rest of his sentence. The feeling of disorientation became measurably stronger, making it difficult to think. Something was wrong, she told herself. Something he had said about Mr. Rose. She had never met the man; why should his name cause this kind of reaction?

"Miss French!"

She jumped and jerked her head up, meeting Paul's impatient green eyes.

"Are you still here, Miss French?"

"Yes . . . yes," she murmured, her voice distracted.

"Well, what the hell is wrong with you?" he asked, watching her in bewilderment and frustration.

"Rose," she whispered hoarsely, her eyes widening as a memory began to grow. "*Rose*. Last night you said you were going to send me a dozen roses."

"And you're sulking because I didn't send them?" He shook his head in disbelief.

She moistened her lips nervously. "And then you said—" She broke off and swallowed heavily. "You said, 'Not roses. Roses make you sneeze.'"

"Then it's a good thing I didn't send them," he said shortly. "Now that we've got that settled, can we please get on with this?"

"How did you know roses make me sneeze?" She stepped closer to the desk, her features tense as she kept her gaze trained on his face. "I *never* told you roses make me sneeze."

He threw the pencil down with suppressed violence. "I've had just about enough of this. Why the devil are you babbling on about roses?" He inhaled deeply, and when he spoke again, his voice was composed. "If it will ease your feeble brain, you did tell me that roses make you sneeze."

"No, I didn't," she said in stubborn confusion. "I know I didn't."

"You did," he insisted tightly, leaning toward her as his anger built. "You told me when—"

He broke off abruptly, a stunned look spreading across his features. He passed a hand slowly across his face; then his eyes met hers with watchful wariness. "You told me when I put the daisy in your hair," he finished hoarsely.

Leah began to tremble. The tremors spread rapidly, shaking her whole body. Her eyes darted around the room as she searched for something solid to hold on to.

"Oh, my God," she whispered. *"Oh...my...God."*

She backed away from him, her movements slow and awkward. Then, without another word, she whirled around and rushed out of the room.

Chapter Six

...do not haunt me thus.

A Midsummer Night's Dream—Act II, Scene 2

Leah raised her face to the sun. As she walked, she lowered her eyelids until her eyes were barely open, so that she could feel more than she could see. The brown cotton sweater she wore with her tan corduroy jeans was light, and the sleeves were pushed up in recognition of the warmth that was at odds with the golden-leafed trees.

The three-acre park next to her apartment building was empty except for a small group of children. The sound of their laughter reached her and made her smile in gratitude. Children's playing and laughing were normal and sane. They somehow helped bring the world back into focus.

Since that first moment in Paul's office, she hadn't allowed herself to think about what had happened, or how it could have happened, or what it would mean to her in the future. She had arranged with one of the other advertising executives to meet with Mr. Rose; then she had walked out of the building without looking back.

For once her apartment hadn't seemed like a refuge from the world. There were too many things there to remind her of the dreams. She had barely had time to change her clothes before the walls began to close in on her.

So she had come here, into the open air of the small park, into the bright daylight and the real world of laughing children. She had no idea how long she had been walking. She simply didn't care.

Leaving the sidewalk, Leah climbed a small rise and sat cross-legged on the grass. Her face was expressionless, her mind free of every thought except the children and the sun shining on her face.

For half an hour, maybe longer, she sat undisturbed; then, on the edge of her peripheral vision, she caught sight of a man walking across the grass toward her. She didn't turn her head to acknowledge his presence, not even when he sat down beside her.

The silence between them lengthened; then Paul said in a quiet, calm voice, "I was driving away from your apartment when I saw you here."

Leah nodded, keeping her eyes and thoughts on the children below. "That little girl with the black ponytail reminds me of my cousin Alta," she said. "She came to stay with us one summer—the summer I was six. For weeks before her visit everyone told me how much I was going to love Alta. She could sing like an angel in heaven and dance like a professional and had already won three Little Miss beauty pageants.'' She paused, then continued in a confiding voice. ''You know, I hated my cousin Alta.''

He laughed. ''That's perfectly understandable. She sounds like the kind of wonder child any normal kid would hate on sight.''

''She threw sand in my hair. That's fair—that's what you do when you're six. But when I returned the favor, you would have thought I had just set the torch to Joan of Arc. I spent the rest of the day in my room and didn't get dessert after dinner.'' She tilted her head to one side thoughtfully. ''Strawberry shortcake, which everyone knew was my favorite thing in the whole world.''

''And were you then more respectful of Cousin Alta?''

Leah straightened her legs and leaned back, resting her upper body on her arms as she gazed up at the small, high-flying clouds. ''I put a lizard down her panties as soon as they let me out of my room.'' She smiled serenely. ''My only regret is that she almost gave the poor lizard a heart attack with her angelic screeches.''

When his soft laughter faded, they fell silent again. She could feel him watching her. She could actually feel his gaze on her face, finding and recording each feature.

"You're scared," he said.

Her laugh was breathless and a little weak. "Aren't you? No—don't tell me. I don't want to know. I don't deal in unreasonable principles, but since I'm being forced to deal in them, it will be the unreasonable principle of my choice."

"And that is?"

"It didn't happen," she said flatly. "I wasn't in your office this morning, and therefore nothing could possibly have happened there. That's the unreasonable principle I choose to accept." She drew a shaky breath. Then, disregarding the unreasonable principle of her choice, she said, "I asked Cooper to take care of Mr. Rose."

There was a pause; then, as though he had decided to humor her for a little while longer, he said, "Yes, I know. Cooper can handle it just fine."

She brushed a lock of hair from her forehead. "I don't think it was the newspaper. I think it must have been the ad agency."

"Most likely," he agreed. "We've had trouble with them from the very beginning, but this had better be the last of it." Leah heard him shift, and when he spoke again, his voice was much nearer. "You know, sooner or later, we'll have to talk about this."

"No, we won't," she said tightly. "We don't have to talk about *this* at all. In fact, *this* is right off my list of things to talk about."

She rose quickly to her feet, and after brushing the grass from her pants, shoved her hands in her pockets. Then, for the first time since he had found her, she looked at Paul. He had taken off his jacket and tie before he joined her. His white shirt was open at the neck, and the sleeves were rolled up, exposing tanned forearms.

Leah frowned at him. He was too casual. It was simply one more thing to throw her off balance, and she didn't like it one bit.

"Mr. Gregory," she said, bracing herself to meet his gaze, "I think I'd like you to leave me alone now."

He didn't stand. He tilted his head back and stared up at her silently, those green eyes still poking and prying, making her uneasy. Then, finally, he spoke.

"I can't be Mr. Gregory anymore, Leah," he said. His voice was so incredibly gentle, it brought the sting of tears to her eyes. "It has to be Paul now."

She bit her lip, then shook her head in violent denial. With awkward movements, she turned and walked away, leaving him staring after her.

Paul watched until Leah was out of sight; then he stood and walked back to his car. His face was expressionless as he drove north toward his own home.

Fifteen minutes later he stood in the large living room, looking around as though it were the first time he had ever seen it. It wasn't the house he had lived in with Diane. After her death he had bought this place, hoping that a new environment would seem less empty. It hadn't worked.

But today it felt different. The atmosphere around him seemed to have a vibrant life of its own. Perhaps because his thoughts were so full, they spilled over and filled the house, too.

He walked into the bedroom and lay on the bed, his hands behind his head as he stared at the ceiling. For a long time he maintained his carefully blank expression; then suddenly he began to laugh.

What a crazy, unbelievable development, he thought. He couldn't even gauge his reaction to it. He was still too stunned, still too incredulous. While he knew there had to be a sane, logical explanation for what had happened, he couldn't forget the way she had looked when he mentioned the daisy. She *knew*. Leah had known exactly what he was thinking about. Because she had been there in that field with him.

He closed his eyes and instantly saw again the two of them lying before the fireplace in the little dream cabin. The smooth satin of her bare flesh was once again beneath his fingers. The sweetness of her mouth lay on his tongue. The warm woman scent of her filled the air, making him dizzy.

Inhaling harshly, he opened his eyes. Definitely a bad idea, he told himself ruefully.

It was difficult for Paul to recall the days when he hadn't dreamed about Leah. Since he had first met her, four years ago, she had been there at night in his dreams. And strangely, even in the beginning, when Diane was alive, he had never felt guilty about those dreams. They were beyond his control and had taken nothing from his wife.

Then, shortly after his wife's death the dreams had changed. They become sizzling scenarios—bits and pieces of blatant erotica. Leah—naked and kneeling beside him . . . leaning close to him so that her hair fell in a golden curtain that enclosed them both...her slender hands on his naked flesh...his lips on the fullness of her breasts...the moans of pleasure that told him she was hot and ready.

When they had first begun, the X-rated fantasies had embarrassed him on wakening. Then he had accepted them as one of the quirks the mind delighted in springing on human beings. There had been no substance to those dreams. Leah hadn't been a personality; she had been unadulterated sexuality.

Then, suddenly, the Roman dream had appeared, and there was Leah. Vital and alive, the real Leah. And in each dream she had become more real to him. She was no longer the cool Miss French who breezed in and out of his office, efficiently taking care of business; she was an exciting individual whose personality had been hidden from him until he had found her in his dreams.

The memory of their ride home in the cab last night was a fuzzy one at best. He couldn't call up actual events, but sensations came through loud and clear. His imagination wasn't that good. Something had definitely happened between them.

He shook his head restlessly. Paul was not a man to give in to weaknesses of any kind, particularly alcohol. But last night, while he had watched her opening up and coming alive for everyone in the conference room except him, resentment had suddenly grown in him. Unreasonably he felt that the dreams had given him rights over her. The vitality and sparkle should have been his alone.

He drew a rough breath, feeling his impatience grow. Sooner or later she would calm down, and they would talk. They had to. He didn't understand what had happened any more than she did, but he knew without a doubt that it was something neither of them could afford to ignore.

Leah sat at her desk, checking through the ads that would run for the next month in financial newspapers and trade magazines. On this level, her job was completely different. There was no ad agency, no creative geniuses to smooth the rough edges. In these ads there were no whispers of exotic locations and exciting wishes fulfilled. These were for the executives who used airplanes the way most people used cars. The purpose of the advertisements was to show that in terms of time and money, it was simply more efficient to fly Universal.

She glanced up as the door opened and Charlotte walked in. She hid a smile. It had been four days since the celebration party, and the brunette's personal crisis had been resolved in the way Leah had predicted, but she could never have predicted the subtle change that had taken place in her secretary. For a reason known only to Charlotte, the sweet, myopic mouse had blossomed. Her expression and posture, even her speech pattern, reflected her new confidence.

"Leah," Charlotte said, "he's called three times already this morning. I told him you were in a meeting, but I don't know how much longer I can put him off. He's getting a little hostile."

"If you think that's hostile, Miss Smith," Paul said as he stepped into the room behind Charlotte, "you've obviously never seen me in action."

Leah stared at him, letting out a slow breath. "It's okay, Charlotte. You can go now."

When the door closed behind Leah's secretary, he said, "You've had more than enough time.... My patience has died a natural death. Are you ready to talk now?"

"No," she said wryly. "But it looks as though I don't have much choice." She leaned back in her chair. "Why don't you sit down, Mr. Gregory?"

When she saw his features tighten, Leah knew she had made a tactical error. Of course he would resent her tone. He wasn't used to receiving even subtle orders, especially from her.

"I'm sorry," she said, biting her lip. "I didn't mean to sound—"

"Hostile?" he suggested as he sat down in the chair across the desk from her.

She smiled slightly. "Yes, I guess that's exactly how I sounded, isn't it? I—" She broke off, placing her hands flat on the desk. "The truth is, this...this *thing* threw me. I handled it badly. Luckily, I'm back on track now."

She wasn't going to mention the sleepless nights she had spent, the hours of confused thought, more hours of reading everything she could get her hands on that had to do with dreams and alternate reality and psychic phenomena, all the trash she had waded through just to get herself back on track.

"I think," she continued, "that because I didn't want to acknowledge that something...well, that something a little strange happened, I let the situation grow out of proportion in my own mind. I made too much of it. Rather than accepting it as a weird coincidence, I saw it as something magic or supernatural—something that doesn't happen in real life."

He listened calmly as she spoke, his expression as steady as always. "But it does happen," he said quietly.

She curled her fingers into tight fists. "Not to me."

Leaning back casually, he studied her face. "'Something a little strange...a weird coincidence'?" he murmured, then shook his head. "You've not only been avoiding me, you've apparently been avoiding the truth as well."

"Whose truth!" she shouted, abandoning her assumed composure. "Are you talking about Jung's truth? Freud's truth? Or maybe you mean Madame Jerinsky the Miracle Medium's truth?"

"Simultaneous occurrences of the same dream are a matter of scientific record," he said, his voice still infuriatingly calm. "They are a fact."

She pushed herself away from her desk and abruptly rose to her feet. "Oh, yes, I know all about it," she said tightly. "I checked out a double arm load of books from the library—probably the same ones you've obviously been reading. But you see—" she placed her hands on her desk and leaned toward him, her slender nostrils flaring with anger "—they don't mean a thing to me. I don't care that twins who live across the world from each other buy identical cars on the same day. I don't want to know about out-of-body, out-of-mind, out-of-pocket or out-of-sheer-bad-temper experiences.''

She paused, sucking in a harsh breath. "And I don't want to hear stupid questions like 'When is reality real?' Don't you understand what I'm saying? What I've been saying from the very beginning? None of that garbage means anything to me. I know what's real, and what you're trying to make me admit *is not real*. I refuse to go off making daisy chains in never-never land. I didn't ask for this, and I don't want it,'' she finished miserably.

He folded his arms, staring at her thoughtfully. "So with a snap of your fingers it disappears...simply because Leah French can't handle it.''

"Yes!'' She grabbed her purse and walked toward the door. "Yes, that's it exactly. I'm glad we finally understand each other.'' She jerked open the door. Then, without glancing back, she shouted, "And stay the hell out of my dreams!''

That evening Leah sat on the couch, staring with unseeing eyes at the bookcase. She shivered slightly and pulled the folds of her dusky-blue robe more closely around her. For hours she had sat in the same position, calling herself all kinds of a fool for blowing up at Paul. She had intended to be so cool, to discuss the situation like a calm, sane adult. Then, the minute he pressed her, her good intentions had gone up in a cloud of smoke.

He would probably fire her, she told herself in resignation. And it was exactly what she deserved. Where was the professionalism that she took such pride in? How could she have screamed like a fishwife at him?

When she heard the knock on her front door, she knew immediately who it was. But it was only when he had knocked for the third time that she stood and walked to the door, standing aside silently as he entered her apartment.

He looked around the room, studying it the same way he studied everything, as though each piece of furniture, each book and painting, was a clue to an unresolved puzzle. When he was seated in an armchair, Leah resumed her place on the couch, curling her bare feet beneath her.

"I'm sorry I acted like such an idiot," she said, breaking the heavy silence. She stared down at her hands. "I don't usually avoid things I don't want to face—I'm not that kind of person." Her lips twisted in a self-mocking smile. "But then, I've never had to face anything like this, so maybe I *am* that kind of person, after all." Bracing herself, she met his gaze squarely. "I'm ready to be reasonable. What exactly do you want to do about this?"

He nodded, as though it was simply another in a long line of predictable reactions and no more than he had expected of her. "I think the first step should be to discuss it openly. Compare notes. Find out what in our separate dreams corresponds." He paused, watching her thoughtfully. "I hate to mention it, but I think we're actually dealing with three dreams."

She let her eyes close briefly, then opened them again, raising her chin in determination. "Yes, I was afraid of that. It started with the Roman dream."

"And then the twenties dream, then the Western one," he said, confirming a fear she hadn't allowed herself to think about. "I've come to some conclusions on my own, but I'd like to hear what you think. Since the first one happened almost five months ago, you must have tried to analyze them before you knew I was having the same dreams."

Pushing her hair back, she stood and walked to the bookcase. She pulled out the three tapes and handed them to him. "Every dream came on a night when I worked late...with one of these running. I didn't pay any attention to the movies, so it took a while for me to realize that the dreams were a replay of the movies."

He examined the tapes, then laughed softly. "I wondered why they were so corny." He glanced up at her and grinned. "Roman soldiers with British accents?"

Leah almost groaned aloud. It was an invasion of privacy beyond comparison. Her instinctive resistance to discussing the situation had been right all along, she told herself angrily. This was much worse than someone reading her mind or peeping through the window while she bathed. The place into which he had intruded was supposed to be inviolable. According to Carl Jung, dreams were the hidden door to the soul. No one—absolutely no one—had the right to invade another human being's soul.

"You're embarrassed," he said, his voice matter-of-fact. "That's perfectly understandable—" He broke off and stared at her hip with a curiosity he didn't even try to hide. "Do you have—"

She jerked her hand to her hip as though he could see her birthmark through the robe. "Yes, I do," she snapped in irritation. "I resent this, Mr. Gregory. I resent it very much." Suddenly her eyes widened in accusation. "And you...you... In the twenties dream—" she sputtered, inarticulate in her anger. "'It's only a dream, Leah. Go with it,'" she mimicked, gritting her teeth. "That was low. That was really low."

"If you'll remember, at that point I thought it was only my dream," he said logically. "And, if it makes you feel any better, I also said and did things that make me uncomfortable to remember."

Slowly, as she recalled the things he had said in the cabin, her anger ebbed. Unwittingly, he had let her see too much of what was beneath the cool mask and, even though he now seemed composed, she knew the whispered words were in the air between them. *My soul was a house where no one lived anymore.* Yes, that would definitely make a man like Paul uncomfortable.

"I think we could say we have enough confirmation to consider the dreams duplicates," he said dryly.

"And where does that get us?"

He was silent for a moment; then he stood and walked to the window that looked out over the park, his face thoughtful. "The dreams were leading us toward something."

Leah moistened her lips nervously. Deep down, she knew what was coming next, but it was another thing she had put off thinking about. "Toward what?"

He glanced back over his shoulder. "Several things—the easiest for me to accept at this time is that they were leading us toward a sexual relationship."

Leah choked on the breath that caught in her throat and began to cough. He said it as though he were talking about filing a report or planting a garden. No drumroll, no pregnant pause—just a flat statement.

"That's the easiest?" she whispered hoarsely. "Then I definitely don't want to know what the others are." She shook her head decisively. "I can't accept that. But even if I agreed with your explanation of what the dreams meant, I think it would be best to just leave it there." She glanced at him, then away again. "For heaven's sake, you're my boss. I can't think of you as . . . as . . ."

"As a lover," he said, nodding absently. "Yes, I see your point. It's easier for me, because I've seen you as an attractive woman for years. Remember, I told you that I'm used to dreaming about you."

Leah felt her heart jerk, skitter along wildly, then settle down again to a dull thudding. She didn't want to remember that. He had told her that in the Roman dream . . . just before her clothes had disappeared, giving her a strong indication of the kind of dreams he usually had about her.

"I'll have to give this some thought," he said, apparently unaware of her reaction. "I can see that you couldn't go into even a brief relationship without making some serious mental adjustments. Maybe we should go away together for a while...to allow you time to get used to me. Then, when you're more relaxed in my presence, we can see what happens."

She passed a trembly hand across her face. "You're going too fast," she said in confusion. "I couldn't...it wouldn't work. The whole time, I would be thinking 'This is Mr. Gregory. This is—'"

"Vulcan? Captain Bligh?" he offered, smiling. "I don't think so. You're an intelligent woman. Once we're away from the office atmosphere, you'll be able to see that I'm as human as you are."

"My imagination isn't that good," she muttered.

He laughed and moved closer. "Oh, I'm human all right. I can prove it to you right now, if you'll let me."

She met his gaze suspiciously. "How?"

"A kiss. That shouldn't threaten you in any way." He took another step. "Nowadays a kiss is almost as impersonal as a handshake."

Oh help, she thought, as hysterical laughter rose in her throat. She stood frozen in horrified fascination, watching mutely as he moved even closer, until he was only inches away from her. Slowly, irresistibly, he lowered his head.

When she felt his warm breath on her lips, Leah panicked and whirled away from him. "I think we'd better talk about this," she said warily, her eyes wide as she continued to back away.

"Miss French!" he said irritably. "Stand still and let me kiss you."

It was a tone that brought an immediate, conditioned response. "Yes, sir," she said.

Before she realized what she was doing, Leah closed her eyes and tilted her head back.

She felt his laughter on her face. "You look as if you're bracing yourself to take a dose of castor oil." His voice was no longer sharp; it was deep and husky... and too damned sexy.

Leah felt his fingers on her neck, clasping it gently. Then there came the whisper of a touch, the soft brush of movement across her lips.

"That wasn't so bad, was it?" he said against her lips.

Leah couldn't answer. She was being taken over by the sudden surge of sweetness flowing through her veins. His mouth found hers again, and this time the caress was more substantial. She felt his firm lips on hers, testing and exploring. Then, when the tension began to build and her breathing quickened, it wasn't his lips or her lips, his tongue or her tongue. It was *their* lips... *their* tongues. Together, they possessed this erotic, pleasure-producing organ.

When he sucked her tongue deeply into his warm, moist mouth, Leah's bones dissolved. She actually felt them turn from solid to liquid.

"That's enough," she whispered hoarsely, pulling away from him.

She could feel those probing eyes on her again, examining her, picking apart her emotions with cold objectivity. Did he see? she wondered feverishly. Could he guess the effect the kiss had had on her?

Closing her eyes, she sighed. Of course he knew. Nothing ever got past him. Ever. Damn him.... *Damn him*.

"That wasn't fair," she said, anger making her voice firmer. "This—" she waved her hand helplessly between them "—feeling between us is nothing more than emotion left over from some damned pornographic dreams. We had a nice, ordinary relationship. We would still have a nice, ordinary relationship, if we hadn't started skipping over the rainbow to Emerald City at night." She raised her chin stubbornly. "I will not allow my life to be rearranged by mirages."

Clenching her teeth to still the aftershocks that were shaking her body, she continued. "So you see, this experiment wasn't necessary. Even if I decided to look at the dreams as some kind of message from beyond, they've stopped. If they were important, if they really meant something, they would have continued. But they didn't. The minute I stopped playing those stupid movies, the dreams stopped."

Her anger fell into a pit of silence. For long, tension-filled moments he didn't speak. Then, when she finally got up enough courage to look at him, he met her eyes squarely. "Yes, they stopped," he said quietly. "But that doesn't make the message any less valid," he said.

He shoved his hands in his pockets and moved toward the door. "You're still afraid. But have you ever stopped to ask yourself what it is that frightens you?

I don't think it's the unusual nature of the dreams that worries you most. No, don't shake your head at me—just listen. I can see that you've put them in the same category as magic or supernatural mumbo jumbo, and you tell yourself that's reason enough to be leery.''

He opened the door and glanced back at her. "But I think what you're really wary of is what the dreams are trying to tell you. You compared the dreams to the fantasy of Emerald City. Why don't you look more deeply into that fantasy? The Wizard of Oz didn't give the Tin Man a heart, Leah. He merely showed him that he had had one all along,'' he finished quietly. And then he walked out.

Chapter Seven

For you, in my respect, are all the world:
Then how can it be said I am alone
When all the world is here to look on me?

A Midsummer Night's Dream—Act II, Scene 2

As Paul paced restlessly around the perimeter of his oversized bedroom, light from the single lamp beside the bed cast shadows on his bare back, highlighting the lean, hard strength of his shoulder muscles.

If Leah had been able to see his face now, she probably would have made some quick mental adjustments. Tonight, the tight control that usually made his features seem so harsh was absent.

Coming to an abrupt halt, he ran a hand through his dark hair. He hated tossing and turning in that damn

bed, but he had to get some rest. There had been too
many sleepless nights lately.

He turned out the light and stretched out on the
bed, but he didn't close his eyes. He lay there, staring
into the darkness, thinking about Leah. Maybe he was
pushing her too hard. He smiled slightly. She had always been stubborn, the kind of woman who liked to
make her own decisions. If he kept pressing her, she
could very well dig in her heels with more determination than ever.

All his life Paul had been the one to make things
happen. He resented not being in control of this situation, and he was impatient with the waiting. There
shouldn't be an empty space in the bed beside him.
Leah should be there.

His eyebrows drawn together in thought, he absently massaged the taut muscles of his neck. Couldn't
she see that their lives would never get back to normal
until they made love? Instead of letting these phan-
tom emotions lead them around willy-nilly, they
should be confronting the situation head on. They
should face it and get it out of their systems, then go
on with their lives. They would be connected by invis-
ible ties until they took steps to break those ties.

But could the ties be broken? he wondered, frowning. Paul didn't want to consider that possibility. He
had taken great care to convince himself that the
dreams were only sexual, and he refused to accept any
other explanation.

He wanted Leah, had wanted her for years. But
there was a long list of complications—good, solid

reasons he had always given himself for never attempting to establish a personal relationship. Since Diane had died, his physical relationships had been limited to women who knew the rules. Tough, sophisticated women who regarded sex as a leisure activity, like tennis or backgammon. There was always one around when he needed sex. And until now that had been enough for him. The whole concept fit nicely into his structured life.

Leah was sophisticated, but she wasn't tough. He knew instinctively that anonymous men didn't float in and out of her bedroom. She would expect more of a man than the women Paul was used to dealing with. That fact alone should be enough to make him back off. But it wasn't. Because the truth was, Paul expected more of her, too. A lot more. With the others he had wanted sex. Now he wanted sex with Leah.

He frowned. That was wrong. He didn't just want to make love to her. He wanted to make love *with* her. He wanted to feel again what he had felt in that little Western cabin. He wanted her to look at him and see someone special.

But since that would never happen, he would take what he could get. God, yes, he would take it, he thought, drawing a sharp breath. Memory of the sweet fire he had felt in her tonight when he kissed her caused his heart to beat faster and harder. Sweet heaven, he couldn't forget the way she had tasted, the way her lips had almost begged for more. He had felt the tension building under his fingers as he held her.

Sooner or later she was going to give in to the feeling. He would make sure of that. He only hoped it was sooner, because he was going quietly insane thinking about her.

A shudder of desire shook him. Rolling over, he punched the pillow and closed his eyes in determination, waiting for sleep to come. Waiting...

* * *

Paul sat at a small wooden table, staring at the hands that were folded in front of him. They twitched slightly, feeling the lack of activity. They were strong hands, hands that were unused to idleness. His clothes were those of a French laborer. Only his boots and the knife he kept hidden in them belonged to Paul, but even the boots had been dyed black so that they no longer resembled army issue.

At that moment he heard a noise outside the kitchen door and instinctively reached down to slip the slender blade from his boot. After rising from the wooden chair, he moved across the room, his steps as silent and stealthy as a white-tailed deer moving through the Texas brush.

Pressing his body flat against the wall beside the door, he waited. When he heard the key rattle in the lock, he lifted the curtain a fraction of an inch and glanced out. Immediately the muscles that had been tensed for action relaxed, and he stooped to return the knife to his boot.

As the woman entered the kitchen, the brief flicker of alarm in her eyes was the only detectable sign of emotion in her face. She glanced at him, then away again.

"Why have you left the basement?" she asked, her voice husky, her French accent pronounced. "You wish to get us both killed? Two streets away from here the sidewalks are thick with Germans." Now the anger in her voice was evident. "If you cannot stay in the hidden room, you must take your chances on the street."

He moved back to the wooden table and swung the chair around. Straddling it, he rested his forearms on the back and watched her as she pulled food from a canvas bag, then filled a metal pot with water and placed it on the stove.

Her blond hair was pulled back tightly from a face free of cosmetics. There was no softness in that face, no attempt to make it more attractive. Her sweater, skirt, shoes and temperament all were a dull brown.

"The rats in the basement only speak French," he said, grinning slightly. "Gutter French. In my one year of high-school French, Mrs. Potts didn't teach us a word of gutter French." He paused deliberately, watching her. "But I understand enough of it to know you won't find a more boring bunch of rodents in all of Paris."

Leah knew he was waiting for a reaction, but she didn't allow her exasperation to show. She didn't understand this tall American who could smile when the world was slowly, inexorably eroding beneath their feet. For one angry moment she wished with all her heart that it had been his Texas the Germans had invaded, that it had been his brother who had been sacrificed to Hitler's unconscionable dream.

Drawing a steadying breath, she walked to the table and, without comment, brushed his hair roughly aside to examine a cut on his forehead. "It is healing," she said flatly. Then, "I've had word."

Paul didn't move, but his green eyes flared with emotion as he studied her face. "And?" he said tightly.

"You must meet them in two days." She paused. "They are good men. If anyone can take you back to your people, these men can."

Paul assumed the men she spoke of were members of the Maquis, the fierce freedom fighters from the hills of France, but he didn't ask. She wouldn't tell him anything more than was necessary for him to know.

He followed her movements as she prepared their evening meal and suddenly began to wonder about this woman he knew only as Leah. In the week he had been in her house, hidden away in a secret room that opened off the basement, she had not let up in her care of him, nursing him through the fever that the cut on his forehead had brought. She knew his body as well as any woman in his life, and still they were strangers. She hadn't volunteered one piece of information about herself or her life, and had asked nothing about his.

He had already come to the conclusion that she wasn't as dull-witted as she appeared on the surface, and as he stared at her features now, he found to his surprise that her facial structure was excellent. At one time she must have been an extremely beautiful woman. If she would ever relax the tight control she was maintaining, not only on her emotions but apparently on every muscle and nerve of her body, she would probably still be beautiful.

"How did you get into this?" he asked, breaking the silence at last.

"The Germans took over my city," she replied, her voice dry. "You might say I was handed a formal invitation to get into this."

"Every Parisian lost his city. It's not unpatriotic to simply stay out of the way. Why did you become involved with the resistance?"

She didn't look at him. She didn't pause in her preparations for the meal. She simply began to speak quietly, in a voice free of emotion.

"My brother René had his fifteen birthday three weeks before the Germans entered Paris. He was as silly and naive as any young man is entitled to be at that age. To René, there were no strangers. Everyone he met was a new friend. The brightness of his mind and his joie de vivre attracted the attention of a Nazi colonel. This man was quick to discover the normal insecurities of youth that lurked beneath the attractive surface. He courted René. He made a young, foolish boy feel important. When René found out he had unwittingly betrayed a friend, he hanged himself."

As she spoke, she chopped the vegetables with smooth, unfaltering motions. "I found him when his body was still warm with the memory of life. I cut him down." The knife came down again and again on the potatoes, the sound unnaturally loud. "I lifted him to his bed and washed him. I dressed him in his Sunday suit. Then I buried him before the Nazis even knew he was dead."

The vegetables were efficiently scooped up and added to the pot that bubbled on the stove. "I am a woman. To take up arms would be ineffective. So I do what I can. I am a small gear in a very large machine. Perhaps the gear will make smoother the process of destroying the destroyer. If the gear sends them to burn in hell even one second sooner, then the small gear has served her purpose."

Beads of perspiration had broken out on Paul's forehead. His white-knuckled fingers gripped the back of the chair with terrible force.

If she had cried, if she had railed against the cruelty of life, he would have felt sorry for her. He would have pulled out worn-out words of sympathy to comfort her. But she hadn't. She had told her story without a hint of self-pity. And Paul had lived every minute of the horror with her.

Neither of them spoke again. They shared the plain but filling meal in silence. Even when he pushed back his chair and opened the door that led to the basement, they didn't speak. Somehow ordinary words would have trivialized what she had told him.

In darkness, he made his way back to the small, hidden room. He removed his boots, holding the knife in his hand as he lay down on the blanket that was spread next to the wall.

In an effort to relax, he tried to call up memories of his home, and the friends and family he had left behind. His world. He thanked God his sister would never have to go through what the woman upstairs had gone through. Leah wasn't even a woman anymore. The war had taken that part of her identity away from her.

When he heard movement on the other side of the panel, Paul rolled to his knees, the knife grasped tightly in his fingers. He saw the glow of the oil lamp seconds before she moved into the room.

"This will keep the rats away," she said, placing the lamp on a wooden crate.

Paul nodded, waiting for her to leave. But she didn't. Without so much as a glance in his direction, she began to undress. She pulled the brown sweater over her head and laid it aside, then unbuttoned the skirt and let it fall to the floor, her movements efficient and without hesitation. As she reached behind her back to unfasten the plain cotton bra, she caught his eyes on her.

"For two years I have been cold and I have been lonely." Her voice was as flat and dispassionate as it had been in the kitchen, but now he saw a slight tremor in her lower lip. "For a little while—just a little while—I want to feel warmth again. For tonight I want to remember what it was like to be alive."

Paul felt an instantaneous reflexive tightening in his loins as he stared at her. The glow of the lamp gave her body soft, hazy edges, reminding him of rich, creamy velvet. There was nothing hard about her now. Her small, firm breasts were proudly beautiful, while the golden-blond triangle between her smooth thighs was at the same time mysterious and poignantly vulnerable.

He had been wrong when he thought her anything less than feminine. As the subtle light stroked the fluid lines of her body, he knew he had never seen anyone who was so very much a woman.

With a casual move, she released her hair to fall around her shoulders, and it was the most intimate gesture he had ever witnessed, sending liquid fire rushing through his bloodstream. At that moment she raised her head and met his eyes. This was not the look of a supplicant. She wasn't begging for his warmth, and she wasn't demanding it. She was simply facing her need with the same strength she had faced the loss of her city and the death of her brother.

Without a word Paul removed his clothes, then spread out the blanket so there was room for them both.

She lay down beside him, keeping her eyes on his face. At that moment Paul knew that something beyond the obvious physical response was happening to him. He didn't just want to give her pleasure, he wanted to bring her back to life. He wanted to give Leah a part of himself, a part that would be with her forever. He didn't want her ever to be cold or lonely again.

He felt her body, barely touching his, and knew as surely as if it had been carved in the stone wall behind him that all his life had been preparing him for this moment, every seemingly random action had been leading him to Leah.

Reaching out, he framed her face with his hands, then slowly lowered his lips to her. For a brief moment she tensed, almost as though his touch were a shock to her system. But when he started to pull back, she grasped his shoulders with strong fingers. She didn't try to deepen the kiss; her lips remained perfectly still beneath his. It was then that he realized she was trying to capture and draw out each separate step of their joining.

Gradually he felt her changing beneath his hands. Relaxing didn't describe it. It was deeper and more miraculous than that. It was like a flower whose petals struggled to unfurl with an almost painful slowness until it at last became a spectacular, open blossom.

When he felt her move beneath his stroking hand, happiness burst wildly in his veins. He had given her this. His touch, his presence, had brought her back to life, back to warmth and light.

She opened her eyes, and they were vibrant gold flames, alive with emotion, blazing with desire. For him. Only for him.

He crushed her close, his urgent fingers grasping her softness. Finally he knew he needed to take as much as he needed to give. Holding him tightly, she laughed, and the sound was pure, unadulterated joy that spread around them and filled every corner of the secret room.

* * *

Paul paced back and forth in the small room. For the first time since he had been there he felt claustrophobic. Something was wrong. Every nerve was screaming at him—*something was wrong*. He had no watch, so he couldn't tell what time of day it was, but he sensed that it was past the time for Leah to be home.

Ugly visions haunted him, driving him mad. The visions weren't nebulous fears; in occupied Paris they were ever-present dangers. Her involvement with the resistance could be discovered at any time. His fists clenched at the thought. What came after the discovery couldn't happen to Leah. It couldn't.

When he could stand the tension no longer, he pushed aside the panel and moved across the basement to the stairs. He didn't stop in the kitchen but passed through the hall to the small parlor at the front of the house.

The wide front windows were heavily draped, cloaking the room in dusky darkness. He stood to one side and slowly lifted the thick fabric to look out. Long moments passed as he simply stared, frozen in one position.

The Germans were no longer two streets away.

Several truckloads of soldiers filled the normally quiet street. They banged on the doors of the houses across the street, accosted citizens on the sidewalk, shouted orders and insults.

As Paul watched, a young soldier repeatedly struck an old man. Again and again he hit him, until finally the old man raised a hand and pointed—straight at Leah's house.

Paul didn't stop to consider what to do next. He knew he had to get out of her house, because the Germans would tear it apart brick by brick until they found him. And then they would wait for Leah to come home.

He raced down to the basement and began moving the boxes into the hidden room, leaving the door open so that it looked like nothing more than an extra storage space.

It took no longer than five minutes, but Paul knew that in those five minutes he had most likely sealed his fate. As he once again entered the hall in the center of the house, he heard the wood of the front door splinter at almost the same instant the glass in the back door was beaten in.

The side alley was his only hope. In the empty room that at one time had been a study, he slid open the window and dropped five feet to the narrow alley. Holding his body against the building, he moved quickly to the corner of the alley that ran behind the house. Ten yards away from him stood the one soldier who remained outside Leah's house. Except for him, the alley was empty, which meant Paul would be noticed the minute he set foot in the open.

Backing slowly, he turned and moved in the other direction. At the other end, where the side alley joined the main street, he moved behind a pile of trash. Then he waited. All he needed was for a vehicle to pass on the street and his movements would be hidden from the soldiers.

Moments later he heard the rumble of a truck approaching from the east and tensed in preparation. When the truck finally appeared, Paul stepped from behind the trash.

At the same moment the young soldier who had been guarding the back alley rounded the corner.

For an instant they both stopped and simply stared at each other; then panic flared in the young man's eyes, and he raised his rifle.

Leah shifted the canvas bag to her other hand. Her steps became noticeably quicker as she thought of the dinner she would prepare for Paul. She wouldn't let herself remember that it was their last night together. One couldn't accept a miracle, then whine because it didn't last forever. A miracle had to be taken on its own terms.

Last night the center of the universe had shifted. Her life no longer revolved around hatred. The center was now Paul and the extraordinary love they had found in the midst of chaos. He had brought back sanity and laughter and love. She knew that even if they weren't together, as long as Paul was in the world, she would never be cold or alone again.

Leah turned the corner onto her street, and suddenly her steps faltered, her fingers clenching the canvas bag. Her eyes grew dark, darting frantically from soldier to soldier. When she spotted a young woman in the window of the house beside her, Leah moved closer.

"They are searching all the houses," the woman said, her eyes red from crying. "They found a radio receiver in Jacques Martine's house. They beat him to death on the street. And André Reneau—" The woman broke off to spit contemptuously on the sidewalk. "He told the soldiers that in a house somewhere on this street, an American is hiding."

Leah felt the blood drain from her face. Dropping the bag, she turned and began to run. She had only one thought in her mind. She had to reach Paul.

The blocks were long. The houses and people around her seemed unreal, as though they had been frozen in place by her fear. By the time she reached her house, her heart was pounding and her lungs were heaving unsteadily in an effort to draw in sufficient oxygen.

Then, behind her in the alley, she heard shots. She ran back, then swung around the corner into the alley and stopped short. For Leah, reality shifted sideways, straightening only because she willed it to.

Paul was on his knees beside a young man. Ignoring the armed soldier, she ran to Paul's side, dropping down beside him, pulling him into her arms, feeling the warmth of his blood on her hands and her chest.

His green eyes met hers, and slowly his lips twitched into a smile. His breath rattled as he inhaled slowly. "My Leah," he whispered, his gaze drifting over her face. "My beautiful Leah."

She could feel him slipping away from her. She could feel the only meaning in her life sliding through her fingers.

"No—you will not die," she said, her voice fierce, her eyes hard with fury. "Do you hear? *You will not die!*"

* * *

"*No!*"

The word was torn from Leah's throat as she jerked upright in the bed. Her heart pounded; her nails dug into the flesh of her palms; her breath came in ragged gasps. Wiping the tears from her her face with rough, awkward movements, she moved to the side of the bed, throwing the cover to the floor in her urgency to turn on the light and locate the address book on her bedside table.

As soon as she found the numbers, she grabbed the phone and frantically dialed in the numbers. Before the first ring had finished, he answered.

"Yes," he said abruptly.

She closed her eyes, pressing her lips together tightly as she gripped the phone. She tried to speak, but no words would come.

"Leah?"

After a moment she whispered hoarsely, "Yes."

She heard his sharply indrawn breath. "I'm all right, baby. I promise you, I'm all right."

She nodded in a short, mechanical motion, then replaced the receiver and slumped down on the bed, deep, dry sobs shaking her slender shoulders.

She had no idea how much time had passed before she heard the knock on the front door. Pushing her tangled hair back, she dragged herself from the bed and walked into the living room.

When she opened the door, she stood and stared at him. Then her face twisted uncontrollably, and he pulled her into his arms, crushing her body against his. The tearing emotions had exhausted her strength. She felt only numbness as she leaned her head against his chest. Without speaking, Paul shut the door behind them and moved with her to the couch.

Holding her next to him, he rocked her back and forth, touching her hair with short, rough strokes. She pressed closer to the warm strength, rubbing her face against the hollow of his throat. After a while, when the strength of his nearness began to penetrate her terror, she felt some of the lingering horror slip away. But still she couldn't move. She wrapped her arms around his waist and held on to the only reality she knew at that moment.

Gradually she felt the world return to normal, and finally she moved away from him. His arms fell to his sides as he watched her.

"Thank you," she said huskily. "I feel better now. What an experience. I will never go to sleep again," she said, giving him a rueful smile. "I promise you, I will never go to sleep again." She shook her head. "I don't understand what happened. There wasn't a movie...I didn't even turn on the television tonight."

"No," he said slowly. "But I did."

She caught her breath. "You did this?" She met his eyes, her face filled with confusion. "Intentionally?"

"No—" He broke off, frowning slightly. "To be honest, I just don't know. I couldn't sleep, so I turned on the television. I don't even remember watching it. I'm certain it wasn't a conscious wish on my part. Maybe somewhere in the back of my mind I wanted to—" He shook his head. "Maybe I wanted to get on with the next step. I don't know. But I would never willingly seek this. I wouldn't put you through an experience like this."

"No—no, of course you wouldn't," she said. "It must have been just as upsetting for you." She shuddered. "This one was different. In all the others, I at least recognized that it was a dream. This time it felt real."

He nodded; then his hand moved to her chin and he lifted it, forcing her to meet his eyes. "If I pull a few strings we can leave today," he said softly.

Leah knew he wasn't asking a question. Because he didn't need to ask. This dream had been the last straw for both of them. She didn't know if she could survive another one. She would do whatever she had to do to make sure there were no more dreams.

A second later, she swallowed hysterical laughter. Who was she trying to fool? There was no place to hide now. The dream had seen to that. No matter how she tried to avoid the truth, it wouldn't go away. Leah wasn't simply attracted to Paul. She loved him. And she probably had from the very beginning.

The very thing she had spent most of her adult life avoiding had sneaked up on her in the dead of night. It simply wasn't fair.

Pulling away from him, she rose unsteadily to her feet. "I hope the place you have in mind doesn't have a television," she said dryly.

"It doesn't matter," he said with complete confidence. "The dreams won't come back as long as we're together. I told you—that's what it's all about."

Sex, she thought, biting her lip to keep from protesting. He thought it was all about sex. And she couldn't tell him how wrong he was. For her, the sexual attraction was only a small part of a larger, unwanted truth. She hadn't sought this particular emotion, and she would be damned if she would simply give in to it.

She would go away with him. And maybe, eventually, they would make love. But she would keep her heart separate.

"Yes, that's what it's all about," she said with quiet determination.

Chapter Eight

The raging rocks,
With shivering shocks,
Shall break the locks
Of prison gates:

A Midsummer Night's Dream—Act I, Scene 2

Leah slid sideways and let Paul help her out of the small Lear jet. Then she stood perfectly still and looked around. At *nothing*.

Rays from a yellow-white sun reflected off the silver body of the jet, momentarily blinding her. And that was the only relief she got from the overwhelming landscape.

Everywhere she looked there were rocks. Large rocks and small rocks; brown rocks and dull beige rocks. There wasn't even a proper landing strip. Heat shimmered in silvery waves from a flat stretch of desert surrounded by towering boulders and jutting cliffs.

Paul had landed them squarely in the middle of hell.

She glanced sideways at him, her expression carefully blank. "I think I've changed my mind," she said slowly.

He chuckled, obviously enjoying her reaction. "Somehow I have a feeling you were expecting a resort condo, with maid service, palm trees and rum punch."

"I don't know what I expected . . . but it definitely wasn't this," she said. Her tone was as dry as the dirt beneath her feet.

It was difficult to believe that only hours ago she had been in the heart of civilization. After they had made the decision to go away together, Paul had barely given her time to pack before he had returned to her apartment. They had driven immediately to a small, private airport.

She hadn't asked questions then, not even when she found out he would be piloting the plane himself. She had been in a sleep-deprived fog, a fog that had overcome her soon after the plane took off.

Now, suddenly, here she was, in the middle of nowhere, with a lot of rocks for company. It was possible she had made a mistake in not asking questions.

She inhaled the sharp, hot air. "Where are we?"

Paul's eyes narrowed against the sun as he surveyed the area. On the surface, he seemed as unemotional as always, but Leah caught a glimpse of something in his face. Relief was the only way she could describe it. As though he found solace in this uncompromisingly desolate place.

"These are the foothills of the Santiago Mountains," he said quietly.

"Which told her exactly nothing. "Texas?" she asked. "Mexico? Chile?" She glanced around. "Mars?"

"We're in the Trans-Pecos region, just north of the Big Bend," he said, and if she hadn't known better she would have said his expression was slightly indulgent. "The Santiagos are a spur of the Rocky Mountains."

"The Big Bend?" she repeated dully, feeling a little stunned. "You're kidding. Nothing lives here—nothing except jackrabbits and bleached bones."

"And us." Reaching behind her, he slammed the door of the plane shut. "At least for the next week," he added, turning to walk away from her.

"Where are you going?" The panic in her voice irritated her as she hurried after him. "You're going to get me in the mood by flinging me into the middle of Dante's Inferno for a week of survival training?" she yelled at his back. "I've been promised trips to New York, Europe and the Bahamas in exchange for my company in the bedroom. If I turned all those down, why on earth—" She broke off and swore, untangling her foot from the low-hanging branches of a dust-covered plant. "Why would I be tempted by a chance to become a Kalahari Bushman? Heavens knows, I wouldn't offend you for the world, but I'm afraid you need a few lessons in—"

What he needed lessons in was muffled against his cotton shirt when she ran abruptly into his back. He turned and looked down at her. The blatant amusement in his eyes made her want to slap his face.

"The purpose of this trip is to let you get to know me, not to get you 'in the mood,' as you so quaintly put it. I can get a response from you anytime I want, anyplace I want," he explained calmly. "But you would resent your response, and I have no use for a brooding woman. When you stop seeing me as your boss and start seeing me as a man, we'll go on to the next step."

As he spoke, her expression went from mild belligerence to narrow-eyed anger, then finally settled down to slightly grumpy resignation. "And I couldn't see you as a man in a green place?" she asked, her smile just a shade crooked. "Somewhere with air conditioning and indoor plumbing?"

"You might see a man there, but you wouldn't see me. This is where I can be myself," he said firmly. Then he turned and began walking again.

"Inflexible, stiff-necked tyrant," she muttered to herself as she followed him. "He can only be himself here.... I should have known he was kissing cousin to an iguana."

When he disappeared behind a large outcrop of rocks, she rushed to catch up. On the other side of the rocks, a Jeep stood under the protection of a corrugated aluminum shelter. Paul was already getting into the driver's seat.

At least it had a vinyl top, she thought as she slid in beside him. Maybe there wouldn't be too many rattlesnakes and scorpions to attack her ankles. Enough heat had penetrated the metal covering and the vinyl top to burn the backs of her legs through her linen slacks, adding to her annoyance.

"Someone forgot to tell this place that it was fall," she said under her breath as she unzipped the clear plastic flap that served as a window.

He turned the key, starting the engine. "A cool front is supposed to come through tonight. It should be down in the eighties by tomorrow."

"And me without my wool underwear," she said sweetly.

Leah felt his gaze on her, but refused to meet his eyes. She knew she was acting like a spoiled child, and she also knew why. She was scared to death.

"Calm down." The gentle understanding in his voice made her jerk her head around in surprise. "Everything will work out just fine."

Leah closed her eyes. He shouldn't know that much about her. He shouldn't know that her temper always appeared when she felt insecure. And today Leah definitely felt insecure. They were here to make love; she couldn't get that out of her mind. But the eventual outcome of their trip was only partly responsible for her edginess. More immediate was the overwhelming physical awareness she had felt from the minute he had picked her up at her apartment. It was as though all the needs and desires she had been suppressing for four years had decided to surface in one violent rush.

And, as if that weren't enough, now it seemed he could read her thoughts.

"If this doesn't work out—" there was a subtle note in his voice that made her turn to look at him "—you can always go home and watch a murder mystery to punish me."

Her lips began to twitch irresistibly. She tried to tighten them, but it was no use. When she caught the sparkling humor in his eyes, she started laughing. Within seconds she felt the tension and wariness and anger slide away from her.

A moment later he pulled the Jeep alongside the plane, put on the emergency brake and stepped out. When she saw him unloading their bags and boxes of supplies, Leah got out and helped him transfer the cargo.

As soon as they were once again on their way, she glanced at him. "How often do you come here?"

"As often as I can since I bought the plane." He jerked on the wheel to avoid a deep rut. "I can usually get one weekend a month here, then three weeks in the spring."

"The plane is yours?" she asked in surprise. "I thought it was a company jet."

His eyes danced with humor, and he gave his head a small shake. "I'm afraid Universal doesn't furnish its vice presidents with private planes yet."

She raised one slender eyebrow. "Maybe not, but they apparently pay very well."

"I have a private income from my father." His green eyes flickered oddly at her as a small smile twisted his lips. "I wonder why that surprises you?"

He was doing it again, she thought in exasperation. Making a determined effort to keep her features free of emotion, she said, "I haven't met a lot of really wealthy people, and most of the ones I've met have been self-made men."

"And the ones with inherited wealth?"

She gripped the seat as the Jeep bounced around a curve. "I dated a man whose grandfather had left him a fortune. He took me to all the best places. He was good-looking, well-bred, charming—and dumb as dirt. His parents gave him everything; there was no need for him to think. Ever. He hired people to do that for him."

"And you decided he was the rule rather than the exception." It wasn't a question. It was a flat statement.

"Why do you say that as though it's exactly what you expected of me?" she asked, her voice puzzled as she turned slightly to examine his features.

He smiled, keeping his eyes on the rough track ahead. "Because it *is* exactly what I expected of you."

"You see me as a narrow-minded bigot?"

"I see you as an individual who, for reasons of her own, prefers not to look beneath the surface. You shelve people in convenient cubbyholes and hold yourself separate from them. You don't want to know about their emotions."

"Nice," she said tightly, resenting his easy assessment of her personality. "And how did you reach those charming conclusions?"

"I recognize those traits because I do the same thing myself." He shrugged. "It's easier...neater. And certainly less unsettling."

She looked away from him, staring at the passing terrain. Not that there was anything out there that she wanted to see, she thought moodily. Once she thought she caught a glimpse of a yucca plant, but it was soon hidden by rock.

She didn't want to look at the scenery. She also didn't want to think about what he had said, but it seemed she had no choice. Leah might resent his reading of her character, but the fact was, he had hit the nail squarely on the head. She did hold herself separate. She hated the thought of being vulnerable. If she didn't let anyone get a foot in the door, they couldn't push the buttons that caused pain.

He said they were alike, but she couldn't accept that. She couldn't believe he had ever been vulnerable, not even where his wife was concerned. She had met Diane Gregory a couple of times. Leah remembered her as a beautiful but ordinary woman. It wasn't difficult for her to imagine that Paul had felt loss at her death, but she knew, almost as though she had looked inside him, that he had never let anyone, not even his wife, touch the deepest part of him.

And no one ever would, she thought with a flash of inescapable intuition. He would never allow anyone to get close to him. That was the knowledge that had been lurking in the background since the moment Leah realized she loved him.

Setting her jaw, she finally looked at the facts. This trip had been exactly the right move. She would prove to herself once and for all that she would never have access to the sensitive loving man she had seen in her dreams.

At that moment the Jeep topped a rise and stopped. After setting the emergency brake, Paul rested his forearms on the steering wheel. Just below them, built on a cliff that overlooked the entire world, was a house.

It didn't stand in contrast to the land—it was a part of it. Made of brown rock, weathered brown wood and huge expanses of glass, the house looked as though it had risen of its own volition out of the solid rock on which it was built. It seemed a natural extension of nature, but a less harsh, less hostile extension.

Here, out in the middle of a landscape only Salvador Dalí could love, was a place that welcomed.

For a long time they were silent; then he turned and met her gaze, a question in his eyes.

"Indoor plumbing," she said in a bland voice.

He laughed softly, sounding pleased, as though something of what she was feeling showed in her face. "Among other things," he said.

Releasing the brake, he let the Jeep drop down the other side of the rise and seconds later pulled to a stop at the front door. Leah opened the door, quickly stepping from the car, and stood surveying the house, taking in the details she had missed at a distance.

"Go on inside and look around while I turn on the generator," he said from directly behind her. "The door isn't locked...no one ever comes here." He glanced at her expectantly, as though waiting for a caustic remark.

"No comment," she said, then grinned and moved toward the entrance.

The front door opened onto an all-in-one living space. It was a high-ceilinged room that seemed to be mostly glass. The wall at one end of the lounge area contained an enormous fireplace made of the same brown rock as the outside of the house. The furniture was shapeless, echoing the colors of the landscape, but touches of navy blue were splashed about the living area, and predominated in the efficient-looking kitchen and small dining area.

Just as the rooms were open to each other, so were they all open to the outdoors. Not a single curtain blocked the view. There was no need for curtains, she told herself ruefully. The only Peeping Toms in this part of the world were probably lizards and bugs.

She heard the soft hum of air conditioning seconds before Paul stepped into the room behind her. He set the bags on the floor and glanced around.

"What do you think?"

"I would be awfully picky if I didn't think it was absolutely perfect. It has a natural feel to it." She waved a hand at the glass walls. "I like those. This way I can get used to the landscape at a comfortable distance."

He chuckled. "Does that mean you're not pining for the resort condo?"

"I never pine," she said, giving him a haughty look. "Since you didn't say a word about where we were going, I was understandably shocked by the scenery. It was like waking up in Two Million, B.C." She walked to the fireplace to touch the cool, rough surface. "I'm sure I'll come to love...um...rocks and dirt."

He tilted his head to the side, a quizzical smile curving his lips. "You're amazing. How could we have worked together for so long without my seeing your sense of humor?"

Leah stared at him. She was still a little stunned by how attractive he was when he smiled. How could they have worked together for so long without her groveling at his feet for attention?

Down girl, she said to herself, breathing deeply to steady her hectic pulse. She shook her head slightly, then stooped to pick up her bags. "Where should I put these?"

He indicated a door at the back of the living area. "That's your bedroom. Why don't you check it out while I bring in the supplies?"

The bedroom was a small blue-and-rust oasis. It had solid walls on three sides, but the rear wall was glass, again with no curtains. The furniture was plain and old and solid...and just exactly right.

She placed her bags on the floor beside the bed, deciding to leave unpacking for later. Finally, after a long, tense morning, Leah was beginning to relax. It was almost as though the house was smiling, urging her to accept and enjoy.

When she returned to the lounge she spotted a box that Paul had placed on the kitchen counter. She crossed the room and began to pull out supplies, opening cabinets to find the right place for everything. Suddenly something she hadn't noticed before caught her eye.

A glass door opened off the kitchen onto a large wooden deck. She slid the door to the side and stepped out; then a small sound of astonishment escaped her. The deck hung right out over the edge of the cliff.

She stood perfectly still, looking out over the barren desert that stretched as far as the eye could see. It was occasionally broken by rocks and decorated by the odd spiny plant and creosote bush.

She heard Paul in the kitchen, but she kept her gaze on the distant view. Moments later he stood beside her.

"Uncle," she said softly.

"Uncle?"

"I give," she explained with a shrug. "I can feel myself actually admiring this place . . . and that scares the heck out of me. This is not my kind of territory at all. But—" she waved a hand toward the distance "—you can't look at that without feeling something. It made me feel small, but at the same time powerful...if that makes sense."

"It makes perfect sense. I feel that way every time I come here. But it's more than that. This place reminds me that I'm a part of it all . . . of the earth, of nature. Sometimes it's hard for me to remember that when I'm stuck in Dallas in a concrete tower. That's why I always come back."

As she listened to him, Leah felt a strange, shivery feeling in the pit of her stomach. This man, not Mr. Gregory but the man who was standing beside her now, could get to her. He could sneak right under her defenses if she let him.

Then, in the blink of an eye, he shrugged off the mood and things were normal again. Leah felt relief, but on a deeper level she also felt regret.

After they had eaten lunch the two of them worked together to clear away the sandy dust that had accumulated since his last visit. It was a welcome period of uncomplicated companionship that lasted for the rest of the day. That evening he grilled steaks for dinner, and they took them inside to escape the insects, eating at the small table next to the windows.

Paul kept his eyes on Leah's face as they ate. This whole scene was nice and comfortable, but it wasn't getting them anywhere, he told himself with a frown. Apparently she didn't feel the same impatience that was setting his teeth on edge. No, he thought, if she felt the way he did, they wouldn't be in the dining room making polite conversation. They would be in the bedroom making love.

"Do your parents live in Dallas?" he asked as he refilled her wineglass.

She shook her head. "They moved to Ohio six years ago to be near my father's sister."

"And the rest of your family? Or are you an only child?"

"I have one brother—John. He's four years younger and lives in San Francisco."

"San Francisco? Is that the reason you're so hot for the promotion?"

She laughed. "I'd want that promotion if I had to move to Yugoslavia, but John's being there makes it nicer."

For the next few minutes there was only the sound of silverware clinking against the pottery plates. Then he said, "Your turn."

She looked up in surprise. "I beg your pardon?"

"We're supposed to be getting to know each other," he explained patiently. "I've asked three questions; now it's your turn."

"What's your sign?" When he gave her a dark look, she grinned. Studying him thoughtfully, she said, "You have no brothers or sisters...and you were criminally spoiled as a child."

He quirked one dark brow. "Have you checked up on me, or are you just guessing?"

"Just guessing," she admitted. "You're uncompromising, which means you had no close siblings, and since you usually manage to get whatever you want, I assume it's a long-standing habit." She paused. "Was I close?"

"I am an only child...and yes, I guess you could say I was spoiled. I can never remember my parents denying me anything I asked for," he said, smiling ruefully. "I'm trying to decide whether or not to be insulted."

"You were painfully honest in your evaluation of my character earlier; I thought I would return the favor. Wait," she continued before he could comment, "I still have three questions coming."

He leaned back in the navy-blue, padded chair, holding a sturdy wineglass in one equally sturdy hand. "I'm not going anywhere. Fire away."

He looked too complacent. Leah felt an irresistible urge to shake him up. "Do you sleep in the nude?" she asked.

He choked on his wine. Several seconds later he said, "You can stop beating me on the back; I'm fine." He surveyed her dancing eyes as she resumed her seat. "You should be boiled in oil for that." He leaned closer. "Besides," he said, his voice low and husky, "you know very well that I sleep in the bottom half of my pajamas."

She had left herself open for that one, she thought ruefully. She wouldn't, however, let him intimidate her. "Dark green silk, if I remember right," she said, her voice perfectly calm. "Okay, next question. Do *your* parents live in the Dallas area?"

"My father is dead; my mother remarried and now lives in Detroit," he answered easily.

"Do you get along with your stepfather?"

He looked puzzled for a moment. "You mean Gerald?" he asked. "I guess he is my stepfather, isn't he?"

"Well, what did you think he was?"

"I don't believe I've ever thought about it one way or the other."

"I'll take that to mean you're not particularly close," she said dryly.

It was yet another example of what she had suspected all along. He was close to no one. If only she could decide whether his emotional isolation was something he actively sought, or if it was simply a part of the character he had been born with.

"What about your father?" she asked, tilting her head slightly to study him. "Were you close? Are you very much like him?"

Paul frowned. How could he answer that? To Leah, Paul probably did resemble his father. Because Paul Harrison Gregory, Senior, had been the most cold-blooded bastard his son had ever laid eyes on. But the resemblance was only a superficial one. Paul's coldness was a shield he had built early in his life. It was a means of protection. His father's coldness had been a character flaw. He had been born with something vital missing. And everyone he touched paid for that defect.

Glancing up, he caught Leah watching him closely. Shaking away the black mood, he smiled. "You're overdrawn. That was your fifth question," he said as he stood and walked to the refrigerator.

Leah stared at his back in frustration. Just when she thought they were getting somewhere, he closed up again. She had been crazy to think for one minute that she could figure out the way his mind worked.

When he turned around, she gasped in surprise. In his hands he held the most elaborate strawberry shortcake she had even seen.

"Where on earth did that come from?" she asked, her eyes wide. "And don't try to tell me you whipped it up when I wasn't looking."

"I had my housekeeper make it while you were packing this morning." He studied it for a moment. "It survived the trip reasonably well."

She shook her head. "I don't believe it." She met his gaze. "You did this because I said it was my favorite, didn't you?"

"I did," he admitted. "I've never claimed to be above resorting to bribery." With a smile of something close to satisfaction, he stared at her laughing face. "What ever happened to dear Cousin Alta?" he asked, placing the cake on the table.

"She's still perfect," Leah said in gloomy resignation. "And I still dislike her intensely. The only difference is that I've had to stop putting lizards down her panties. Alta is married and lives in Dallas now. Her family moved there when we were both in high school . . . the same high school," she added darkly.

When he handed her a huge piece of the cake, she used her index finger to scoop up a big blob of whipped cream. "Oh, that's wonderful," she breathed, her eyes closed. "And this is still my favorite."

"Did Alta give you a tough time in high school?"

"Only when I let her. Back then I was still jealous of her. She needed an extra room for all her clothes." She met his questioning glance. "In high school, clothes came right below boys on the top-ten list. Alta had both. And I will never forgive her for latching on to Teddy Bowers. It was nothing less than blatant thievery."

He leaned his elbows on the table. "Was Teddy important?"

"Captain of the basketball team," she said, daring him not to be impressed. "It wasn't really the fact that she got Teddy; it was how she did it. Our group had planned an unofficial senior trip—it wasn't school-sponsored or anything—to Colorado for a week of skiing. *Everyone* knew he was going to ask me to go steady on that trip. He had been leading up to it for weeks. Then I tripped over my brother's skateboard and broke my ankle."

"And while you were recuperating Alta made off with Teddy," he said, his eyes sparkling with enjoyment.

"The little sneak promised to let him touch her breasts if he would give her his senior ring," she said with wide-eyed indignation.

"You weren't prepared to...uh...match that offer?"

"No!" she said, then grinned. "To tell you the truth, I couldn't have even if I had wanted to—Alta is stacked. What I can't forgive is the way she rubbed it in for years afterward."

"It's a wonder it didn't put you right off skiing."

"It would take more than the loss of a skinny basketball player to do that," she said firmly. "I managed to make it to Aspen the next winter and probably had a much better time on my own."

"Aspen? That's where I used to ski. It's getting too crowded these days." He frowned. "Your senior year, you said?" She nodded. "That would have been . . . about nine years ago?"

"Almost exactly."

"I was still going there then. Let's see, nine years ago. That was the year they had the big jazz concert."

"That's right," she said eagerly. "That's another thing I regret about missing the trip. We had reservations at Holbiens, where they were holding the concert."

"You mean your group was there that week?" He looked surprised.

"Yes . . . why?"

He smiled. "That was the week I was there."

"You don't mean it," she said, her eyes sparkling. It was almost like running into an old school friend. "Where did you stay?"

"At a chalet not a quarter of a mile from Holbiens. Wait a minute," he said, frowning thoughtfully. "A group of kids . . . wearing blue baseball caps with orange letters."

"Those were my friends!" she said, her voice rising with excitement. "I can't believe it. Why on earth would you remember them?"

"They disrupted the concert by singing 'If you're not from Texas, you're pond scum' to the tune of 'Yankee Doodle,'" he said dryly. "How could I forget?"

She threw back her head and laughed. After a moment she tried to catch her breath, darting a look in his direction. "I wrote the lyrics," she confessed, her lips twitching.

He groaned. "I should have known."

She leaned back, sighing. "Nine years. It doesn't seem like that long. I still can't believe you were there."

Paul glanced away. It hadn't occurred to her yet, he thought. If she hadn't broken her ankle, they would have met nine years ago. Before he met Diane. Before a meaningless marriage had dulled his emotional outlook. Maybe it was only a strange coincidence, but somehow he didn't think so.

"I cried the whole time they were gone," she said softly, shaking her head. "I never could understand that. I had been looking forward to the trip, but it wasn't a matter of life and death. It wasn't even Teddy. I had already decided to turn him down when he asked me to go steady." She frowned. "But I can't remember every crying so hard. There was a strange ache in me that wouldn't go away." She drew a deep breath. "I guess it was because I knew my childhood was almost over."

Paul didn't say anything. He couldn't. He was too wrapped up in memories. More than one night during that ski trip he had drifted in that strange place between waking and sleeping...and he could have sworn he heard someone crying. The minute he came fully awake it went away. He had forgotten about it until this moment.

Standing abruptly, he began to clear the dishes, willing his hands to stay steady. He felt Leah's gaze on him, but didn't meet it. He was acting totally out of character, he told himself sternly. He had to pull himself together. But he couldn't do that with her watching his every move.

She stood. "Let me do that," she said. "You did the cooking."

"I'll do it," he said, his voice sharper than he had intended. Glancing at her, he said, "You're probably tired. Why don't you go to bed?"

Leah stared at his stiff features for a moment, her brow creased in bewilderment. She wasn't tired, but it was his house. If he wanted her to be tired, who was she to argue? And that was a dismissal if she had ever heard one.

"Well . . . yes, I guess I am ready for bed." She hesitated, waiting for him to say something, to do something. Anything. But he simply continued clearing the table. "Good night," she said stiffly, and turned away.

In the small bedroom she slowly took off her clothes and slipped into her gown, then got into bed.

Thirty minutes later she sat up abruptly. This was crazy. Why should she let him get to her like this?

Because I love him.

No, she told herself firmly. She didn't love him, she loved the man she had met in her dreams. She loved that part of Paul that he would never allow anyone to see. It was there; she knew it was there. But it was guarded by a wall so strong that it could never be torn down.

There would be nothing but pain for her if she allowed her love for him to flourish. She had to cut the living emotion out of her heart and mind before it began to grow. Then she would be safe again.

She couldn't let him play with her emotions the way he had been doing since the minute they had discovered they were having the same dreams. He had said he wanted her to get used to him, but that wasn't what he had in mind at all. He intended to tease her with false glimpses of a softer side until she was willing to go down on her knees to reach that part of him.

Well, it wouldn't work, she decided, raising her chin. She refused to play his game. She would take things into her own hands and break the spell the dreams had cast on her. And she would do it now, before he had a chance to hurt her.

She slipped from the bed and walked to the door. Without giving herself time to back out, she moved into the lounge. But it was empty, and so was his bedroom.

When she began to tremble in relief, she clenched her fists and moved toward the kitchen.

Moonlight played on the wooden deck, turning the whole world silver. Paul was lying back in a lounger, his head turned away from her toward the desert. Her bare feet made no detectable sound as she moved, but seconds later he tensed and jerked his head in her direction.

He didn't speak. Not even when she sat beside him on the edge of the padded lounger. But as he stared at her, the flesh across his cheekbones tautened, and a muscle flickered at the corner of his mouth.

"I'm comfortable with you now," she said flatly. "There's no need for us to wait any longer."

Reaching out, she grasped his neck with strong, slender hands and leaned down, pressing her lips to his.

The moment they touched, he seemed to surge beneath her, as though something had exploded inside him. He dug his fingers into her shoulders and jerked her against him roughly. It was as though he had pulled a switch to release a dazzling, sensual current. He whispered words she couldn't hear as his lips moved across her face to her throat.

Shock widened her pupils, her senses flaming as she strove to reach for a distant sanity. She seemed to be in a state of hypersensitivity. The soft moonlight blinded her; the gentle night sounds echoed loudly in her ears; the silk gown scraped roughly against her flesh.

The intensity of her reaction caught Leah off guard. Quick, piercing stabs of sexual excitement shot through her body, and without a whimper the disciplined suppression of years disappeared without a trace. She lay beside him on the lounger, her mind completely given over to pleasure.

This wasn't the way it was supposed to be. She had sought him out for the Act, not this violent, compelling explosion of sensation. With Grady, her one and only experience, it had always been the Act. How could she have guessed that it could so different? So amazingly wonderful?

He framed her face with big, awkward hands, and his intense gaze penetrated her solid flesh, seeming to reach to the heart of her.

"Do you know?" he whispered hoarsely. "Do you have any idea how badly I want you? How many years I've wanted you?" He inhaled roughly. "You couldn't. It would scare the hell out of you if you did. It scares me."

A small sound escaped her, and against her volition, her face moved against his hands. How would those same hands feel on her breasts, on her thighs? she wondered. Instant, electrified heat shot through her body at the erotic thought.

As though he had once again intercepted her thoughts, a groan emerged from deep in his throat, and his fingers tangled roughly in her hair, bringing her lips back to his. He plunged his tongue into the sweet, moist cavern of her mouth in an act as intimate, as possessive, as the one they both desired. She wound her arms around his neck and returned the kiss with a hunger that quickly grew unmanageable.

His hands began moving feverishly over places that had been too long neglected. Seconds later he rolled with her in his arms until she was beneath him. Then, cupping her breast, he lowered his head and teased it with his tongue through the thin fabric.

"This is what I lie awake nights thinking of," he said in a grating whisper as his hand slipped intimately down the curve from her breast to her thigh. She heard his breath quicken, and it brought a pleasure beyond belief. "The feel of you. The taste of you.

The look on your face when you hurt to have me inside you.''

She moaned, grasping his hard buttocks with shaking fingers as she surged upward. A harsh sound caught in his throat, and he thrust his knee between her thighs.

Oh, yes, she thought frantically. *Yes ... please.*

Suddenly, without anything to warn her, he tensed, muttering unintelligible words under his breath. Then, as though moving against a dragging force, he pulled away from her and sat up on the edge of the lounger.

For a long time Leah merely lay there, shuddering in reaction. She focused on the sound of his harsh, irregular breathing as though it would somehow bring her back to sanity. When the effects finally began to recede, she moved to sit up, her hands clasped tightly in her lap as she waited for an explanation.

"Sorry," he said, breaking the strained silence. "I'm afraid I got a little carried away."

"That was the idea," she said, her voice as dull as her senses.

He shifted away from her, as though something about her disturbed him. "You got a hint just then of how badly I want you. So you'll understand that it's not easy for me to say this." He glanced at her. "It's all wrong," he said flatly. "Something just doesn't feel right."

Leah felt hysterical laughter rise in her throat and cut it off sharply. "I'm afraid this is all I've got," she said, shoving the disheveled hair from her face. "Which part of me is it that 'doesn't feel right'?"

His laugh was self-mocking, but also contained irritation and an emotion she couldn't identify. "Every part of the outside of you feels just exactly right . . . maybe too right."

"My insides are wrong?"

Her voice was openly flippant. It was the only way she knew to put distance between them, to control the fire in her body that still threatened to get out of hand.

"Don't be dense," he said tersely. "You know what I'm talking about. It's not the right time for this."

"As an excuse," she said slowly, "that ranks right up there with 'I've got a headache' and 'It's the wrong time of the month.'" She cautiously met his eyes. "I don't understand you. We came here to—" She broke off abruptly and glanced away from him in acute discomfort.

He smiled slightly. "You can't say it, can you? But right now, that's exactly what it would be. And that's why we can't let it go any farther tonight. Try to understand me—if I wanted a nice, friendly roll in the hay, there are hundreds of woman I could go to."

Some quirk of the moonlight made his face look sad, almost wistful, as he continued. "But no dream would lead me to them. That's not what the dreams are about."

"Hundreds?" she echoed, then whistled under her breath in admiration. "Your little black book must be the size of the Dallas yellow pages." When he didn't comment, she stood abruptly and swung away from him. "Your delicate principles are a little difficult to believe. You were the one who said this was all about sex." She shook her head restlessly. "I don't know what you want from me. What is it we're supposed to find up here? Some kind of timeless, everlasting love? A star-crossed destiny?"

"Maybe."

The word was a whisper that barely penetrated the silence, but to Leah it seemed as loud as an erupting volcano—and just as dangerous. Before she could recover from the shock, he began to speak again.

"I just don't know," he admitted wryly. "I'm as much in the dark as you are. I only know that what we started tonight wasn't it . . . not yet."

She couldn't respond. How did one respond to insanity? That softly spoken "maybe" was way outside the realm of reality.

Inhaling slowly, she turned away and walked into the house. She left needing him, hating him. And loving him more than ever.

Chapter Nine

I know a bank whereon the wild thyme blows,

A Midsummer Night's Dream—Act II, Scene 2

Leah felt a slap on her rear and wiggled in protest, pushing her head deeper into the pillow. She was popped again, this time with enough force for her to feel it through the cover.

"Come on, lazybones. It's time to get up."

She moaned and rolled onto her back, opening one eye to stare up at the man standing beside the bed. With the one eye that was open, she examined him. The gray sweatshirt he wore had seen better days. The sleeves were only a ragged memory, exposing the full length of his tanned, muscular arms. Tight, faded jeans molded his hips and thighs.

"Who're you?" she asked thickly.

He chuckled, leaning down to place a hand on either side of her head. "I'm a new day," he said. The bright, cheerful note in his voice set her teeth on edge. "I'm the harbinger of wonderful things to come."

"You're an escaped lunatic," she said warily as he straightened away from her.

What new mood was this? she wondered as she sat up. It was as though her miserable attempt at seduction the night before had never happened. Which suited her just fine, she thought grimly. But even if he had decided to have a convenient memory lapse for the sake of diplomatic relations, that didn't explain the way he was dressed, or his jolly mood. It was on a par with Prince Charles pretending to be a good old boy.

She didn't understand it, but that couldn't prevent a tingle of excitement from attacking her sleep-numbed limbs.

"Abby used to pour a glass of cold water on me when I wouldn't get out of bed," he said.

She didn't trust the look in his green eyes. "Who's Abby?" she asked, pushing the tangled blond hair from her face.

"My nanny."

Leah gave an inelegant snort. "No one in Texas has a nanny."

"I did. And she taught me something very important."

"What's that?" she asked. Her lips curved upward in a bemused smile as she stared at his twinkling eyes and animated expression.

"She taught me that a day without cold water splashed in your face is a joy to wake up to."

She laughed huskily, then glanced toward the glass wall. "Was it my imagination, or did it rain last night?"

"It rained."

"Where are the puddles? The morning mist?"

He moved toward the door. "This ground drinks water almost as fast as it comes down." He looked back at her. "Come on, move. Breakfast is getting cold. And wear something rugged. We're going to explore the world today."

As soon as he was out of the room, she pushed back the cover and scrambled from the bed.

Five minutes later she walked out onto the deck. Paul turned toward her, a piece of toast halfway to his mouth. He closed his mouth abruptly and stared at the designer jeans that were the color of ripe wheat and the pale rust, short-sleeved blouse.

"When you decide to get rugged you don't hold back, do you?" he said, shaking his head. "That outfit's perfect for backpacking around Beverly Hills."

She sat down beside him at the table and began to fill her plate with bacon and scrambled eggs. "It was either this or a pink, rhinestone-studded jumpsuit," she said in unconcern. "Someone forgot to tell me to bring clothes suitable for roughing it. But even if I had known, I couldn't have matched that." She waved a piece of bacon at his sweatshirt. "What did you do— mug a street person?"

He caught her hand and took half her bacon in a single bite. "This is my lucky sweatshirt."

"It's lucky it's not dipped in gasoline and used to clean auto parts," she agreed.

She listened with pleasure to his deep laughter as she swallowed the sweet orange juice. For some reason the world seemed to be sparkling this morning. There was an intoxicating freshness to the air. The colors of the rocks seemed sharper and clearer.

"Are you through?" he asked with obvious impatience.

She rose to her feet, then picked up the plates from the table and carried them to the kitchen. "Am I making you late for an appointment?"

"Yes." He took the plates from her, quickly shook the scraps into the sink, then shoved the dishes into the dishwasher. Picking up a canvas knapsack, he grabbed her hand. "Now, let's go," he said, pulling her toward the front door.

It closed behind them, the sound muffling whatever he was saying.

"What?" she said, following helplessly along behind him. "I can't hear you."

"I said I wish you had decent shoes."

She glanced down at her canvas tennis shoes. "What's wrong with my shoes?"

"Nothing, if you're playing tennis, but they haven't got much grip to them."

When she jerked her hand out of his, he stopped walking and turned to look at her. "Why do my shoes

need grip?'' she asked slowly. "What do you intend
for them to hold on to?''

A slow grin curved his strong lips. "The side of a
mountain."

It wasn't actually as bad as he made it sound. For
the rest of the morning they explored the sloping
country around the house. Gradually she came to
know and accept the stark beauty of the land. Paul
showed her dozens of different plants, explaining in
his quiet voice how each managed to survive in the dry
climate. They saw strange, intricate rock formations
that towered above the landscape, and deep ravines
that cut through it. As the morning passed she not
only felt a growing fascination for the land, she also
felt it for the man beside her.

Hours later they sat on a ledge shaded by an over-
hanging rock. The sun's rays made the air a white-hot
screen between them and the rest of the world, fading
the brightness of the morning.

She glanced at Paul. "What's in the knapsack?''
"Lunch.''

Scrambling to her knees, she grabbed the bag. "I
was hoping you would say that,'' she said eagerly, and
began pulling out the food.

Either the air or the exercise had given Leah an ap-
petite. She couldn't remember ever being so hungry.
As they ate, they talked lazily of the things they had
seen that morning. Then talk died away, and they
leaned against the rock in easy companionship.

"No matter how many times I look at that," she said, staring out across the landscape, "I always see something different."

"So do I. And I've been coming here for years." Shifting his position, he repacked the knapsack, then glanced at his watch. "Our lunch has had time to settle. How tired are you?"

She sat up straighter. "Not at all," she said, her answer surprising her. "This morning has been very basic, hasn't it? It gave me—oh, I don't know—I guess a sense of power describes it best. Definitely a sense of accomplishment. I suppose it appeals to the part of my brain that's left over from prehistoric days. There are no artificial, man-made complications here. Just us and nature."

She caught his grin and laughed. "That will teach you to ask me a question. I didn't mean to go into a monologue, but I've really enjoyed this."

"Good," he said, rising to his feet. "Let's go."

"Where?"

He lifted his eyes to the rock face behind them. "Up."

The next two hours were the most challenging of Leah's life. When he'd said up, he'd meant straight up. To an experienced climber the ascent would have been a snap, but to a junior executive, city born and bred, it felt like scaling Mount Everest.

After a while, when she felt the strength begin to drain out of her limbs, Leah kept going because she didn't want to disappoint Paul. Then suddenly she began to climb because she didn't want to disappoint herself. Perspiration ran down her face, stinging her eyes and blurring her vision, as she scrambled for hidden footholds in the rock face. Her knuckles were scraped, her fingernails broken, her feet and knees bruised. But she refused to give up.

Several times he paused, his face blank as he watched her progress and waited for her to catch up. His face might have been blank, but he watched her with such intensity that she knew his thoughts were full.

The world had been reduced to one section of the mountain, and she became totally obsessed with straining every muscle to move the next few feet upward. Each time she pulled herself up to the next level, Leah knew the next move would be the last she could possibly make, but somehow she managed that one last move again and yet again.

She was vaguely aware that Paul had disappeared over a ledge five feet above her. But when he spoke, his voice startled her.

"Just a couple feet more, and then I'll pull you up," he called down to her.

"No—" Her voice was a hoarse whisper. She clenched her teeth together. "I . . . can . . . do . . . it."

She had long since forgotten why it was important; she only knew that she had to do it alone, without his help. Drawing up her bent knee, she planted a foot on a small jutting rock, then used the foothold to push herself upward. Two more feet covered. Two less to climb.

Minutes later the ledge was under her fingers. She found a small crevice with her foot and pushed up, straightening her arms against the rock surface. Now the top half of her body was above the ledge. Paul was on his knees beside her, waiting and watching.

Drawing in a deep breath, she slung her right leg over the edge and heaved herself up and over. Then she collapsed full-length on the hot, flat rock. She was there.

Leah couldn't think. She could only lie there and force stinging air into her lungs. She didn't open her eyes, even when she felt him pick her up and move her into the shade, keeping her in his lap when he sat down.

When it stopped hurting to breathe, she opened her eyes and looked up at him. The pain was receding, and the triumph began a slow explosion inside her. Suddenly she began to laugh. She laughed uncontrollably, hugging him, spreading kisses across his hard, dirt-streaked face.

As though he understood, Paul rocked back and forth with her in his arms and laughed, sharing her triumph.

After a while she shifted in his lap and pulled at her perspiration-drenched blouse. "Paul, this is disgusting. We're sticking together."

When he didn't say anything, she glanced up at him. "What's wrong?"

"That's the first time you've ever called me Paul," he said quietly. Smiling, he stood up and set her on her feet. "Now, are you ready to throw your arms around my neck and give me much adulation?"

"Sorry," she said, shaking her head. "I never adulate even in the best of circumstances, which these are definitely not."

"Never say never." He placed a hand on her shoulder and turned her around.

Leah blinked, her mouth opening, then closing again in amazement. The rock platform where they stood was cut deeply into the side of the mountain, and there, in a sheltered corner, was an oasis.

With a mere whisper of sound, a thin curtain of glistening water slid across boulders, collecting in smooth basins hollowed out of solid rocks. Some held a scant cupful of water, some were as large as bathtubs. But it was the main basin that drew her eye. It was at least twelve feet across, and deep. Around its edges, in crevices and tiny alcoves, plants grew lush and green.

"Paul," she whispered in awe. "Oh, *Paul*." Swinging around abruptly, she threw her arms around his neck and kissed both sides of his strong jaw.

"Are you, by any chance, adulating?"

"I'm adulating like you've never seen anyone adulate before." She hugged him. "It's *paradise*. We climbed the 'steep and thorny way' and reached heaven."

His eyes shone as he glanced from her to the pool and grinned. "Ready?"

Seconds later they ran into the water. They played and splashed like two kids playing hooky. Eagerly they washed away the dust, letting the water soothe their cuts and scrapes. It felt like a healing place.

It was much later when they climbed out and stretched out on the smooth rock, letting the sun dry the clothes on their bodies.

Paul lay on his stomach, resting his head on his folded arms as he studied the clean, smooth lines of her profile. There was a strange feeling of singularity about today, the same subtle impression of sensual innocence that must have existed in the Garden of Eden. They could have been the first man and the first woman, before the cares of the world made them ordinary.

After the scene on the balcony the night before, he had decided he couldn't wait any longer. He would have to take things into his own hands and forcibly bring about a closer relationship between them. That was what today had been all about. In this setting and under these circumstances, the stiffness of their past association had to slip away. Here they were just a man and a woman.

Leah, he thought, smiling slightly. Woman of iron. When he had recognized the gritty determination in her face as she pulled herself up the cliff an inch at a time, he'd thought his heart would burst from sheer pride. A woman in a million. Soon to be his woman in a million.

"That blouse will never be the same," he said, running his gaze over the torn, stained garment.

"Ask me if I care." When she stretched her arms over her head in a slow, lazy movement, her fingers brushed against a fern. "I can't get over this place. It's like something out of a fairy tale."

He sat up, folding his legs Indian-style. "The waterfall is only here because it rained last night," he explained. "That's why we had to come today. The big basin is deep enough to keep water in it during the dry spells, but the little ones dry up fast."

"So the plants are here all the time? I'm glad." She turned her head toward the fern. "What is this?"

"Maidenhair fern. Behind you is a columbine. And this is creeping thyme." He broke off a leaf and handed it to her. "Crush it between your fingers to release the oil."

She looked up at him. "You're rich. If you didn't have a nickel, all this would make you rich. It's got to be the most beautiful place in the world."

Tilting his head back, he stared at the wide expanse of sky. "Put this place in a park in Dallas and you wouldn't even notice it. It's special for two reasons. The first is that it's here against all reason. You go along thinking rocks and cactus are normal and fitting; then this happens, and it's almost a shock to the system—a piece of beautiful unreality."

Leah's brow creased in thought as she studied his somber face. She sensed somehow that he wasn't only talking about the water hole.

"And the second reason?" she asked softly.

He glanced down at her and gave a slow, teasing smile. "The second reason it's so special is that we had to work so hard to reach it. The best things don't come to you without a struggle."

"You know," she said, her voice thoughtful as she rose to her knees, "I'm learning not to trust that smile. What are you up to?"

He reached out to flick the tip of her nose with one finger. "The question is, what are *you* up to? Are you up to another climb?"

"More?" She glanced around. The sun was already dropping low on the horizon. "It's getting late. Hadn't we better start back now?"

"We've got time. I know a shortcut back."

For a moment she was silent, then she said slowly, "Do you mean you made me climb that mini Mount Everest when there's a shortcut?"

"Are you sorry?"

She relaxed her shoulders and smiled. "No," she said quietly. "No, I wouldn't trade the experience for anything." She rose to her feet. "Okay, my simple but trustworthy native guide, lead the way."

She followed behind him as they made the easy climb up the boulders beside the waterfall. Their destination, approximately thirty feet above the water hole, was a fifteen-foot-wide natural balcony that jutted out from the mountainside. Here was the source of the waterfall: a shallow basin overflowing with collected rain.

"Come over here," he said, keeping his voice low as he lay flat on his stomach at the edge of the rock balcony.

She stretched out beside him. After a moment she whispered, "What are we doing?"

"We're waiting."

Leah smiled. Yesterday she would have questioned him, or at least made a smart-mouthed comment. But this was today. And today was different. She was different. The man beside her was different.

Will the real Paul Gregory please stand up? she thought whimsically. Which one was he—the rigid vice president of marketing, the vulnerable, gentle-hearted man of her dreams, or the strong, complicated being beside her now? Maybe he was all three.

"Look."

The word was only a whisper on the wind, but when it reached her, she followed his gaze to the oasis below. Animals were gathering to drink. Mice and birds, goats and deer, shared the watering place. She held her breath when a spotted cat crept close to the basin. The other animals didn't run, as she had expected. They continued to drink, but Leah could almost feel the watchful wariness in them.

She touched Paul's shoulder and mouthed the words "Mountain lion?"

His eyes flared with sudden humor. Turning slightly on his side, he held his hands several inches apart. "Bobcat," he whispered. Then he spread his hands several feet apart. "Mountain lion."

She gulped, glancing over her shoulder at the crevices behind them. When he put his arm around her waist and pulled her closer, she could feel him shaking with silent laughter.

Leah didn't mind. He could laugh at her forever, and she would still forgive him—because he had shown her this. It wasn't the same as watching ani-

mals in a zoo. She felt a kinship with the animals below, almost as though she could think what they
thought and feel what they felt.

After a while Paul scooted back away from the
edge, gesturing for her to follow. When his movements wouldn't disturb the animals, he stood and
helped her to her feet.

"You're just full of surprises, aren't you?" she said,
still keeping her voice low as she smiled up at him.
"You've given me some wonderful gifts today—it's
like digging through a treasure box, pulling out one
jewel after another."

"Are you ready for one last jewel?" he asked, gazing at something behind her.

Leah turned around and froze in her tracks.

The world was on fire.

Ordinary rocks were splashed with orange and red,
bronze and gold. As far as the eye could see in any
direction, the landscape was alive—majestically,
spectacularly alive—with blinding color.

It was the climax of Tchaikovsky's *1812 Overture*.
It was the Vienna Boys' Choir singing *Te Deum*. It was
a John Donne devotion.

Slowly she turned to face him. "This is it, isn't it?
This is the place that looks like the day the earth was
born, the place that feels like forever."

He didn't answer. As his gaze drifted over her face,
he raised a hand to her cheek, his long fingers splayed,
his palm cupping her chin. "You've turned to gold,"
he whispered huskily. "Golden hair, golden eyes. I

could be struck blind tomorrow and still see your eyes."

His hand tensed slightly on her face, then he dropped it to his side and looked away from her. "This area is one of the few places where geologic processes are so clearly shown that even an untrained person can understand them." His voice was matter-of-fact as he gestured outward toward the rugged terrain. "Those rocks reveal the history of the earth for the past one-hundred million years. Not quite forever, but almost." He paused. "We'd better start back now."

The swiftness of the change in his mood confused her. She felt as if she were being bounced around like a rubber ball. What kind of game was he playing now? One minute he seemed to be showing her something of the man behind the mask; the next he slammed a door shut between them.

As they followed a gradually sloping trail downward, she told herself that she had no right to expect anything else from him. He had never promised her a soul mate. The only purpose of their trip had been for her to loosen up around him. For her to see him as a man, rather than her boss.

It was logical, but all the logic in the world wouldn't wipe out the memory of the way she had reacted to him back there. He had no right to manipulate her emotions that way.

"We'll have to climb down now." He had stopped a few feet in front of her. "About fifteen feet below here there's another ledge that will take us the rest of the way down. Since descending is a little trickier than ascending, I'll go first and give you directions to the footholds." He stared down at her, frowning. "Do you think you can manage it?"

She stiffened when she caught the doubt in his tone. "Of course I can manage it." She glanced at the sky. "What about you? Are you sure you can see the footholds? There isn't much light left."

"I know every inch of this place," he said, his voice abrupt. "Just do what I tell you and we won't have any problems."

Arrogant bastard, she thought as she watched him begin the climb down. "Now you," he called from just below her. "That's right. Two feet to the left you'll find a small cleft in the rock."

She moved slowly downward under his steady stream of directions. Going down wasn't as tiring as going up, but it gave her a terrible feeling of insecurity. She didn't like not being able to see where she was going.

"Eighteen inches directly below your right foot there's a protruding rock." He made an impatient sound. "You're swinging to the left—I said directly below."

She glanced down. "Wait," she said. "I see a place." She moved her foot farther to the left.

"No, don't—"

But his warning was too late. The rock crumbled and disappeared from beneath her foot. Looking down had thrown her off balance, and the abrupt movement jerked her hands loose from their hold on the cliff. In a futile effort she grabbed at the rock as she began a rapid descent. Seconds later she hit the narrow ledge below with enough force to bounce her sideways. And over the edge.

This time her frantic fingers found something solid—the branch of a small bush. She felt a thorn pierce her palm, but she didn't have time to feel the pain, and even if she had, she couldn't let go. There was still a twenty-five-foot drop below her.

When she heard a sliding noise above her, she glanced up. He was there, grasping her wrists, pulling her up to the narrow ledge. She leaned against him, her breathing rough and shaky.

After a while the paralyzing fear began to recede, and she realized he was holding himself so tense that his flesh felt like steel beneath her fingers. She pulled away to look up at him, catching a glimpse of some strange, indefinable emotion before he shut his eyes. When he opened them again they were blazing with fury.

He dug hard fingers into her shoulders. "I told you to follow my directions." The words were thick and sluggish as though they were being forced out of him. "If you had simply done what I told you, this wouldn't have happened."

Leah stared in amazement. She had never seen him so angry. The fiery temper he showed at the office was nothing compared to this. He was trembling with the intensity of it. Suddenly he gave her one hard shake that snapped her head back.

"Don't you ever—"

"Stop it!" She jerked away from him and scooted backward. "No one treats me like that," she said hoarsely. "No one. I've spent a lot of years getting to a place—an emotional level—where no one can treat me like that."

She glared at him in bitter anger, her fists clenched, and the words wouldn't stop. "I didn't follow your directions because I don't depend completely on *anyone*. I take care of myself. If I want to do something stupid, that's my business. I make good decisions and I make bad decisions, but they're all *my* decisions. I am not a meek, obedient female, and I refuse to pretend I am." She stopped to drag air into her lungs. "If you can't accept that, then *stay out of my way*."

Long seconds passed, and the silence stretched out between them. Paul was staring at her as though she had sprouted another head.

Leah closed her eyes and leaned back against the rock. He had a perfect right to look at her like that, she thought wearily. She had overreacted—something she seemed to be doing a lot lately. Even as she had said the words, she knew they were stronger and harsher than the situation had warranted. She also understood why.

For just one moment, under the blazing sunset, Leah had wanted to beg. She had wanted to say she would do whatever he wanted and be whatever he wanted if he would just love her. And that knowledge made her sick to her stomach.

"Are you ready to go?" he asked quietly.

She nodded and slowly pulled herself to her feet.

An hour later she sat on the side of the bed in the small bedroom. She had bathed and tended her wounds and changed into decent clothes. Now it was time to go into the living room. She couldn't stall for much longer. Sooner or later she would have to face him.

Later, she thought, as she walked into the lounge and found it empty. Walking through to the kitchen, she began to prepare dinner. After a few minutes he joined her. But he didn't speak. He simply moved around, setting the table, helping her with the food.

When they sat down to eat, "Pass the salt" and "Would you like a beer?" were the extent of the dinner conversation, but she could feel him watching her, and it was driving her crazy. After fifteen minutes he set his fork down with a thud and pushed back his chair.

"Are you through?" he asked, his voice carefully polite.

"Yes."

"Then leave the dishes. I'll do them later. We need to talk."

She followed him to the couch and sat down at the opposite end. He stared at the empty fireplace for a moment, then turned to her. "That outpouring of bitterness—that wasn't about your fall and my understandable anger. That was about another man. I don't like that."

She drew in a slow breath. "You don't like it. Is that supposed to make a big difference to me?"

"I'll rephrase my statement," he said, his lips twisting in a wry smile. "Another man presents a complication we don't need. We have enough problems without that. We agreed this is something we have to do. I think the question of whether or not you're involved with someone is relevant to our situation." He paused. "Is it Yarrow?"

She blinked in surprise. How did he know she was seeing David? Feeling his gaze on her, she shook her head. "You're wrong. I know I overreacted out there, but it wasn't about another man. It was about me."

He waited, expecting more. And Leah knew he wouldn't let up until he got it.

"It's a boring story," she said irritably. "You don't really want to hear it."

"Why don't you let me decide that for myself?"

"Oh, for heaven's sake." She shot him an exasperated look. "I had a bad affair in college; I was infatuated with a dictatorial phony. It taught me some things about myself that I needed to learn, but it left a few scars. Up there on that ledge, I was upset. I reacted to a memory, not to you. I'm not upset now, so it really doesn't affect 'our situation.'"

He studied her features. "What did it teach you about yourself?"

"That I'm not the kind of woman who can handle love or commitment . . . or even an emotional involvement, for that matter."

She could almost see the gears turning in his head. She was a puzzle that he would solve, even if he had to dissect her brain to do it.

"You haven't been involved with anyone since college?"

"Once was enough," she said, then smiled wryly. "You don't have to make it sound as if I'm a freak. I simply chose the kind of life I wanted."

"No involvement." The words were speculative. "And yet you're a healthy woman with all the right responses—I would even say more responsive than most. Which means sexual relationships without emotional entanglements. Somehow, I would have said you wouldn't enjoy that type of thing." He frowned. "I suppose I miscalculated."

She almost laughed. He sounded annoyed, as though a formula had gone awry.

After a moment he glanced at her sharply. "Or did I?"

She shifted her position, smoothing the fabric of her slacks with one hand. "I can't see that it's any of your business."

There was another heavy pause. "It must be...what, four or five years at least since your college affair?"

"Eight."

He whistled under his breath. "It must have been more than an infatuation to have that kind of effect on you."

She turned, meeting his eyes. "Is this necessary? I've already explained that none of this has anything to do with Grady. Did you really think I've been pining away for lost love? I told you, I don't pine. This is about *me*. When I was involved with Grady, hidden pieces of my character began to surface, pieces I didn't like. Because I thought I loved him—no, that's wrong. Because I wanted him to love me, I let him walk all over me. I started changing to suit Grady's idea of what I should be."

She leaned her head back, her lips twisting in self-contempt. "Would you believe I even dyed my hair red? Padded bras, tight skirts—whatever Grady wanted. But that wasn't the worst of it. The worst is, I stopped laughing. I acted like a dim-witted dullard. Oh, I know what you're thinking. You're thinking I should simply look for a man who likes me the way I am, but that's not the point. The point is, by not standing up for myself, I gave Grady permission to use me as a doormat. I can't even say that I realized what was happening and broke off with him because of it. I didn't even think of leaving him until I found out he was sleeping around."

She frowned, brushing the hair from her forehead. "Sometimes I wonder what would have happened if he had been ashamed of himself, or sorry that he had hurt me. That really frightens me. Because I'm afraid if he had, I would have stayed with him."

She clasped her hands in her lap and stared at them. "Now do you see why my policy of noninvolvement is only about me? When you find out you can't handle alcohol, if you're smart, you stay away from it. I decided to be smart."

"It makes sense," he murmured, then glanced up. "Not your conclusions. They're stupid. But your past shows in the person you are now. It all fits together."

She raised one slender brow in inquiry. "My conclusions are stupid?"

"Stupid," he confirmed flatly. "You were a different person then—not as strong. You didn't have the solid sense of your own identity that you have now."

"Can you guarantee that it wouldn't happen again?" she asked, meeting his eyes. "Of course you can't. Logic doesn't have anything to do with emotions. The thing I always come back to is this—my affair with Grady was an overblown teenage crush. And look what happened. I won't take a chance on something that goes deeper." She sighed. "Unfortunately, I have to have something on which to base a physical relationship. You were right about that. There should be something—friendship, respect . . . even a strong physical attraction would do. But there has to be more than just desire to mate with any available male."

"And in eight years you haven't found a single man who you were strongly attracted to?" he asked in disbelief.

Just one, she thought, glancing away from him. "Can I help it if I'm particular?" she hedged.

He was silent for a while. "As your boss," he said slowly, "I think I've earned your respect."

His voice was completely casual, but for some reason she had to swallow a nervous lump in her throat. "I can't think of anyone I respect more."

He moved closer. "And up there at the water hole, that felt like friendship."

"A lot," she whispered hoarsely. "It felt a lot like friendship."

His body was next to hers now, almost but not quite touching. When he reached out to tilt her head upward, her eyelids drooped as a strange weakness overtook her.

"That leaves only one thing," he whispered, his voice deep and husky. "Are you at all attracted to me?"

She moistened her suddenly dry lips. "As a matter of fact, I am."

His thumb stroked her cheek. "Then may I make love to you, Leah?"

A rough sound came from her throat, and she closed the two-inch gap between them, finding his lips by blind instinct. Instantly he slid his arm under her knees and stood up to carry her to his bedroom.

All the rules for a first sexual encounter were thrown out the window the minute they fell on the bed together. Their clothes were tossed aside as quickly as they could manage to shed them.

Some other time they could have gentle, romantic passion. But not tonight. They had waited too long for each other to wait one more minute.

There was no hesitation or awkwardness between them. Leah touched the warm flesh of his body and felt that it belonged to her, had always belonged to her. She opened beneath him freely and naturally, as though this fiery loving had always been a familiar and beloved part of her life.

The instant Paul was inside her, she felt—beyond the intense pleasure—a curious lightness, as though a weight had been removed. Their loving was as basic as the country seen through the glass wall beyond the bed. There were no sophisticated, practiced moves between them. It was hunger meeting hunger. Need responding to need.

Then, suddenly, the sunset was there in the room with them, cannons and all.

For a long time afterward Leah felt she had lost the use of her muscles. Paul's spectacular brand of loving had turned her into a jellyfish. A lazy, contented jellyfish. As she waited for the delicious lethargy to disappear, she listened to the sound of Paul's rough, shallow breathing.

"Leah?"

"Mmm?"

"I take it that was a yes."

She laughed, a breathless, satisfied sound. "Should I have said the words? Yes, Paul, you have my permission to make love to me. In fact, you may do it as often as you like."

His teeth nipped gently at her smooth shoulder. "I think I'd like that in writing." He slid his hand down her hip, then sat up.

"What are you doing?" she asked.

"Something I've been aching to do for months." His self-mocking laugh had a strange intensity to it. He turned her slightly, then leaned down and kissed the rose-colored, Persian-lamp-shaped birthmark.

It was crazy, she thought. A simple touch and she was on fire again. When he buried his face in her stomach, she groaned, reaching for him as the miracle began again.

Much later, while he slept beside her, Leah lay awake staring into the darkness, knowing without a doubt that she had just made the biggest mistake of her life.

She hadn't expected this. She felt different, totally different. How could it have changed her to this extent? The depth of the feeling frightened her. She couldn't let this happen to her. After this week they would go back to what they had been before. Or they would have an affair. Could she accept either alternative?

She turned her head to look at him, and her muscles tightened in reaction. God, she loved him. She would crawl over hot coals to get to him. She would willingly, eagerly, do all the things she had sworn she would never do again.

And none of it would do her any good. Because none of it would buy his love.

Reaching out, she touched his face with an unsteady hand. At least she would have this week. For this week she wouldn't worry about the future. For this week she would let her love for him have its own way.

Chapter Ten

Ay me! for aught that ever I could read,
Could ever hear by tale or history,
The course of true love never did run smooth:

A Midsummer Night's Dream—Act I, Scene 1

The stars are so crowded up there," Leah said softly, her head against his shoulder as she gazed upward. "There's almost no room for sky."

Paul shifted on the lounger, pulling her closer. "That's why they put the McDonald Observatory in this area. There's no glare from city lights, and the air is so clear you can see a hundred miles in any direction."

Leah tilted her head slightly upward. This was the only direction she wanted to look. It was Saturday night—the last night. Tomorrow they would go back to Dallas.

Quickly, she pushed the thought away. Instead she thought back over the past week. Their time together hadn't been magic, or a fairy tale brought to life. It had been exciting, down-to-earth reality. Each moment had been packed full of life, especially the moments in each other's arms.

And each moment—day or night, laughing or loving—Paul had watched her with the same expectant intensity as he had when she had climbed the rock face.

"It must be a shock to come to the city and see our measly handful of stars."

He bent down and tucked the blanket around her feet. "I remember when all that was up there was the moon and the stars," he said thoughtfully. "Now there are black holes and quasars and pulsars and supernovas—"

"That's enough," she said, laughing. "No wonder it's so crowded up there. If it keeps going like this, Earth will have to move to the suburbs." She snuggled against him under the blanket. "I love your mountain, Paul. And your house, and even your rocks and dirt. I'm glad you brought me here...not only because the dreams will stop now, but because it's a wonderful place. A place I didn't even know existed."

He didn't say anything, but his arm tightened around her waist, and she knew he was pleased.

"What do you really think about those dreams?" she asked thoughtfully. "How could something like that have happened?"

Paul ran his hand over her arm, studying her features. Tonight she was a silver enchantment, sent to entice him. When he didn't answer, she turned to look at him, and he smiled simply because she was beautiful.

"I don't know. But I know there's nothing in them to be afraid of. The human brain is largely unexplored territory. All we have now is a lot of garbled information that has led to half-formed, usually worthless theories. Someday we may be able to fully understand what the mind is capable of, but not now. From what I've read, people who experience these simultaneous dreams have some kind of strong emotional connection." His lips twisted in a rueful smile. "Although you aren't tied to me emotionally, we run on the same wavelength; we think and feel alike. We have all along, without ever knowing it. Something in our makeup matches."

So, she thought dully, with a few words the passion that overwhelmed and the love that overflowed were reduced to a genetic foible.

Don't think about it, she told herself. Not tonight. Not while there was still a minute of their time left.

She lifted her head, her nostrils twitching suddenly. "What is that? Every time a breeze comes through I catch a whiff of the most gorgeous smell."

"It's cereus."

"I smell a cloud formation?"

He chuckled. "Not cirrus. Cereus. Night-blooming cereus. It's a cactus. They're rare and inconspicuous, which makes them almost impossible to find since they only bloom at night, but it's the most beautiful of all cactus flowers. It opens at sundown, then closes again at daybreak. And you can smell the perfume a quarter of a mile downwind."

She slid her feet to the side. "Let's go find it."

"Whoa," he said, pulling her back. "I don't think so."

"Why not? If they're that hard to find, it would be like finding a unicorn."

He leaned his head back, exhaling in a soft gust. "Some things you have to accept as impossible to find. You know it's there—it makes its presence known just enough to tantalize, just enough to torment. But it's always out of reach." With the moonlight on his face, he looked as cold and unreachable as a gray marble statue. "That's when you have to decide to take what you can get. Enjoy the perfume, and don't look for something of more substance."

Standing abruptly, he walked to the railing that ran along the edge of the deck. "We have to go back tomorrow," he said in a voice devoid of emotion.

Why did he have to remind her? she thought restlessly. She had taken great care not to think about it.

He turned around. "Have you enjoyed this week?"

Leah felt the sting of tears in her eyes, but stubbornly blinked them away and smiled. "I've loved every single minute of it." That much she could tell him.

"I'm glad. Leah, I've done a lot of thinking this week. A lot of hard thinking. I've come to the conclusion that since we've been here, we've given each other things we couldn't have gotten from anyone else. With you, I'm not so rigid. It's easy to laugh when you're around. And when we make love—"

He broke off, and his eyes finished the sentence, sending a flash of pure lightning through her veins. "We make magic together," he said softly. "For me, a great deal of the pleasure comes because when we make love, you see *me*. You want *me*, not just a physical release. That's the kind of woman you are. But because that's the kind of woman you are, and although you have a very sensual nature, you've neglected that part of yourself for a long time." He exhaled a long, slow breath. "And that's what I've given you. With me, you can be all that you were meant to be."

He rubbed his temple in an unconscious movement. "I've never believed in fate. The idea goes against the grain with me. But I can't help thinking about that ski trip you were supposed to take. I can't help thinking that we should have met nine years ago."

Leah glanced away from him. That would have been before his marriage, maybe even before he met Diane. Would it really have made a difference?

She sighed. Maybe it really was written in the stars that the two of them should get together. But not forever. She had already accepted that. If this thing between them was meant to be, it was most likely to teach them something about themselves. Leah hadn't decided yet what she would learn from the experience. Perhaps she was going to find out how much pain she could take before she broke.

She deliberately made her voice light. "Nine years ago I was a silly teenager. You were already a grown man. And even if you had been attracted to me, you aren't the kind of man to propose an affair to a teenager."

For just an instant he stiffened, almost as though she had touched a nerve. "No," he said, his voice barely audible. "No, I wouldn't have done that."

Silence fell around them, growing heavy with tension. What was this all about? she wondered, her fists clenching. Why the postmortem? Whatever it was, she wished he would get it over with. She didn't think she could take much more.

Although it had been her wish, when he spoke, the sound of his voice startled her.

"I have a proposition to make."

His voice was firm and strong now. She had heard this particular tone hundreds of times in the past, in conference rooms and business meetings. Paul had had years of experience at hiding his thoughts. He was a master at it, she thought with resigned wistfulness.

"I don't want you to give me an answer now. Take your time and think about it." He turned away, looking out over the moonlit desert. "I think we should get married."

Her pupils dilated in shock, and she became as still as a statue. For a stunned moment she couldn't think;

she felt dizzy. She heard his next words through the faint buzzing in her ears.

"I know this is coming at you right out of the blue," he continued, "but I think we could make it work. Even if we discount the dreams and the physical side of our relationship, we've still got more going for us than most people have. We're alike, Leah. Our priorities are the same—hell, we even think alike." He paused, letting his argument sink in. "Will you think about it?"

She swallowed heavily. It felt as if hands were squeezing her throat. "Yes—yes, of course I will."

Leah couldn't look at him. Her gaze wandered aimlessly around the deck. She was trying to decide how she felt, and suddenly realized she couldn't feel anything. That almost made her laugh. Her brain felt the way her lips did when she went to the dentist.

Had he just proposed a merger? she wondered in confusion, then shivered violently.

"You're cold. Let's go inside."

When she stood, he took the blanket and walked beside her into the house. Even inside, she still felt chilled. When her teeth began to chatter, she threw him a rueful glance. "Maybe you should light the fire."

His movements full of controlled violence, he threw the blanket onto the couch and jerked her into his arms. "Maybe you should light a fire. Here, in me. Kiss me, Leah," he said, his voice rough and husky. "Kiss me and watch me burn for you."

Then there was only his touch. No pain. No decisions. No confusion. There was only the way he made her feel.

On Monday morning Leah walked into the outer office and paused to look around. This had been her world for so long, but even this world looked different now.

"Did you enjoy your vacation?"

She glanced at Charlotte, her eyes widening slightly. Here were more changes. Her secretary had a whole new look. New hairdo. New clothes. The glasses were gone, and her eyes were a brighter shade of blue.

"Yes, I did," Leah said. "Very much. I like your new look. You're very pretty, Charlotte."

The brunette looked pleased. "Thank you." She held out her left hand, displaying a diamond engagement ring. "What do you think?"

Leah felt a tiny, pricking pain in her temples, but she pushed it away. She wanted to be pleased for Charlotte. She lifted one slender brow. "Do I know him?"

"It's Lester."

At last something managed to pierce the fog of confusion that had been with her for the last twenty-four hours. That single word brought her back to life with jolting force.

"Lester?" she choked out.

Charlotte nodded, a mischievous twinkle in her newly tinted eyes. "When you have time, drop by his office. Lester is a changed man. I think I finally managed to get him straightened out."

Leah's lips twitched uncontrollably, and seconds later the two of them burst out laughing.

A short time later, when she walked into her office, Leah didn't examine it the way she had done the outer office. Blood was finally flowing in her veins again. She didn't want to know that this, too, was different.

She had laughed with Charlotte. Life continues, she thought with a sigh. She wasn't really going to fade away for lack of love. As she had told Paul, she didn't pine.

The day before, when he had dropped her at her apartment, she had asked him to give her the coming week to think about his proposal. She needed the time away from him so that she could think with some measure of objectivity.

She leaned her head back. What a laugh, she thought, mocking herself. How could she be objective when her very life was on the line? When Paul was near, she couldn't think because of his nearness. When he was away, she missed him too badly to think.

Just then the telephone buzzed, startling her. Shaking her head to clear it, she leaned forward and picked up the receiver.

"Mr. Leighton is on line one," Charlotte said.

The head of personnel? she thought, frowning. She didn't need personnel problems today. "Put him through."

"Hello, Leah," the older man said when he came on the line. "Did you have a nice vacation?"

"Yes." Her voice was brisk and unencouraging. How many times was she going to have to answer that question. "What can I do for you, Ed?"

He laughed. "You're very cool about this. But there's no need for us to beat around the bush. You got it, Leah."

For a moment she had no idea what he was talking about. Then she dropped abruptly into the vinyl chair, a look of blank surprise on her face. She had gotten the San Francisco job.

She wasn't surprised at the promotion. It was her reaction to it that shocked her. A month ago the San Francisco job had been the most important thing in her life. She had worked herself half-crazy for it. But all that seemed to have happened to someone else. Someone Leah no longer knew.

"That—that's wonderful," she said weakly.

"They wanted you out there immediately," he continued. "But I told them you would need at least a month to clear things up here. That should give you time to fly out and find a place to live and get all your work in order."

Leah responded automatically to the rest of the conversation, her mind whirling wildly. When she replaced the receiver, she leaned forward, resting her head on her folded arms.

Life was so contrary, she thought. Her love for Paul had made everything else seem trivial.

Somehow she managed to get through the rest of the day. But the night was another proposition entirely. She barely made it through the night. She ached for

Paul; she needed him desperately. Not only his love-making. She needed the warmth of his body beside hers, the sound of his voice in her ear, the look in his eyes when he laughed.

As she moved through the days, she tried to think. She honestly tried. But at the back of her mind there was always the compelling urge to pick up the telephone and tell him that she would marry him whenever he wanted.

She recalled what he had said about the sweet-smelling, night-blooming flower. Could there be a lesson in that? She told herself that she would be stupid not to settle for what she could get from him. Wasn't a little better than nothing at all? Surely having part of Paul was better than having any other complete man.

At that point in her tangled thought processes she would reach out to call him, but something always stopped her. The same thing went on for three tense days. And three interminable nights.

On Thursday evening she lay on the couch, staring into the darkness, as the deep silence began to close in on her. She had put it off long enough. It was time to think about all the things she had been avoiding.

What scared her most? she wondered. Was it the fact that she loved him too much, or the fact that he didn't love her at all?

Could she enter into a marriage, given either of those two facts? If she did, what would she be like in a few years?

Visions rose in her mind, making her flinch. Visions of an endless, aching need. Visions of the bitter, lonely woman she would become. She would eventually come to hate Paul for being himself. For not being able to love her. And he would lose every ounce of respect he had for her.

She wouldn't do that to herself. She couldn't do it to him.

Yes, she thought, staring at a shadow on the ceiling, that's the answer. She had finally reached a decision. There was no wavering in her now. There was nothing in her now. Everywhere there was only emptiness.

Minutes later a knock on her front door startled her out of her self-absorbed mood. Sitting up, she switched on the lamp at the end of the couch, then walked across the room.

"Hello, Leah," Paul said quietly when she opened the door for him.

"Hi," she said, glancing away as she wiped the palms of her hands on her robe. "I didn't expect you."

"I can tell," he said wryly. "I know you said you wanted time alone to think." He seemed edgy and uncharacteristically restless. "I meant to stay away, but all evening I've had the craziest feeling. I can't explain it. A kind of coldness." He shook his head. "Maybe this is what getting old feels like." He smiled slightly. "I didn't know it would hit before I'm even forty."

He walked away from her, running a hand through his hair. "I didn't even know I was coming here until

I pulled into the parking lot. I thought I was going for a drive, just to get out of the house."

Swinging around abruptly, he met her gaze. Suddenly no more words were necessary. The need was achingly clear in his green eyes. She moved quickly to him, putting her arms around his waist to hold him tightly.

"You don't have to explain," she whispered, her fingers digging into his back as he lifted her to carry her into the bedroom. "I don't think I could have made it through tonight without loving you."

One last time, she told herself. Then she gave herself up to desire.

At dawn, when he rose from the bed to leave, Leah kept her eyes closed, pretending to be asleep. She felt him stroke her face, and his touch crucified her with its gentleness. Then he turned away and quietly left the room.

This couldn't happen again, she thought. Each time they made love, it was more difficult to imagine life without him. Each time attached her more firmly to a man who didn't want that kind of attachment.

Never once had he mentioned love. He had some crazy idea that they were destined to be together, and he was acting on that idea, rather than any real desire to marry her.

For Leah, it just wasn't enough. But she would have to break away from him soon. Because if she didn't do it soon, she wouldn't have the strength to do it at all.

Later that day Leah sat stiffly at her desk. It had taken some maneuvering, but everything was set. Her bags were in the car. She had arranged to take another week of vacation. She would stay with her brother in San Francisco. Maybe she would look for an apartment while she was there.

This was necessary, she told herself. She needed the distance to reinforce the decision she had made the night before. In a week she would feel stronger. Then she would come back to Dallas and make arrangements for the move.

Right now she had a letter to write, she thought, picking up a pen.

It wasn't long, and it wasn't complicated with emotions. In the letter she simply told him that marriage was not for her. She wanted the San Francisco job because her career was her life. Knowing him and working under him had been an experience she would never forget.

The last part was the only truth in the entire letter.

Leah knew she was running away. She simply couldn't see that she had any other choice. Paul could change her mind without even lifting a finger. And that would be disastrous for both of them.

Reaching out, she picked up the telephone and buzzed Charlotte. "I need you to make a reservation for me on the next flight to San Francisco International," she said stiffly. "Bump someone if you have to, but get me a seat."

Charlotte gasped. "Leah, I can't do that. Not even the chairman of the board bumps."

"Do it, Charlotte. I want to be on that flight."

Replacing the phone, she waited, her face blank. Five minutes later Charlotte confirmed that she had a reservation on Universal's one o'clock flight to San Francisco.

Rising slowly to her feet, Leah picked up her purse and the sealed envelope, then walked into the outer office.

"This is for Mr. Gregory," she said, handing Charlotte the letter. "I want you to hold on to it until this evening, then give it to him before he leaves the building. I would rather he didn't know until then that I'm going out of town."

The brunette nodded slowly. "Leah, is something wrong?"

Leah smiled. "I hope you have a wonderful life with Lester, Charlotte. You were right; he's changed."

"We'll be fine as long as I don't take my foot off his neck," Charlotte said, her gaze still trained on Leah's face. "But you—" She broke off, tears forming in her eyes. "I don't know why... you look the same as always, but something's different."

"I got my promotion. Associate vice president, Charlotte. What else could I possibly want?" She turned and walked toward the door, then paused. "Please don't forget the letter to Mr. Gregory."

"No, I won't.... Goodbye, Leah."

Paul sat at the conference table, listening to one of the directors speak. He didn't hear the words. He couldn't get last night out of his mind. Why had their lovemaking felt so desperate? He had never seen her like that. She had seemed on the verge of breaking.

Was it something he had done? he wondered, his fingers tightening on a pencil. Or something he hadn't given her that she needed?

Maybe what she needed she couldn't get from him. He didn't want to think about that. How could she be so absolutely right for him when, by every indication, he was so obviously wrong for her?

There were very few things in his life that Paul hadn't been able to arrange to suit himself. When he ran across a problem, he fixed it. In the past it had been just that simple. Why couldn't he fix this? Why couldn't he break down the barrier she had built around herself?

Suddenly the room felt airless and a strange tightness gripped his chest. *Something was wrong.* The thought was as clear as if someone had spoken it aloud. Paul felt panic shake through him. Something was wrong.

He stood up and walked out of the conference room, unaware of the astonished eyes that stared after him.

He took the elevator down to the next floor. He didn't stop in the outer office but walked straight to her door. He already had it open when Leah's secretary spoke.

"She's not here, Mr. Gregory."

Paul turned slowly to face her. "When will she be back?"

"She's gone for the day."

The brunette looked nervous as she avoided his eyes. He stepped closer to her desk. "Where is she? Has she gone home? Is she all right?"

"She's not ill," Charlotte said, casually moving a paper to cover something on the desk. "She just decided to take the rest of the day off."

Bending slightly, he picked up the paper before Charlotte could stop him. Beneath it was an envelope addressed to him—in Leah's handwriting.

"When were you supposed to deliver this?" The words sounded thick and dull to his own ears.

"Tonight, before you left the office," she said, biting her lip.

He stared at the letter for a moment, then slowly picked it up and walked into Leah's office, closing the door behind him. His face held no trace of emotion as he ripped it open and began to read.

Leah shoved her flight bag into the overhead compartment, then took her seat. Turning her head, she looked out the window at the smooth concrete. Men were moving around the plane, loading luggage and food. But Leah didn't see them. She focused on the glass, and instead of seeing her own reflection there, she saw Paul's.

She glanced quickly away, drawing a deep breath. John would pick her up at the airport. It had been almost a year since she had seen him last. She would find out what was new in his life and let him show her the sights over the weekend. Then, on Monday, she would go to the Universal office at the airport. Tuesday she would start checking the newspapers for an apartment. She would settle in quickly. Leah had always been an adaptable person.

Who are you trying to kid? she asked herself as she slumped in her seat. Adaptable? When had she ever tried to adapt to hell? When had she had to adapt to having a part of her soul cut away.

At that moment she caught a glimpse of a man three rows in front of her and her pulse went crazy. The back of his head looked just like Paul's. Suddenly the man turned, and she felt a dizzying disappointment spread through her. He didn't look anything like Paul.

Would she measure every man she met in the future against Paul? she wondered. Would they all be shorter or taller, heavier or lighter, than he was?

It will get better, she told herself, wiping the film of perspiration from her forehead. This was real life. Emotions faded. Maybe the pain would never go away, but someday she would get used to it.

Paul stared at the freeway ahead, his knuckles white on the steering wheel. His facial muscles were stretched tight, accentuating his bone structure.

Every move he had made since reading the letter had been an automatic response. He didn't even know what he planned to do if he got there in time. She had made her decision; why couldn't he leave it alone?

Because it would be easier to lose a hand, he thought dully.

In the four years they had worked together, they hadn't had a personal relationship. He hadn't tried to get closer to her. But he had known she was there.

Maybe he could live without being married to her. Maybe he could get on with his life without their ever making love again. *But she had to be there.* He had to know that Leah was in his small part of the world. He had to be able to see her, to hear her laugh.

How was he going to accomplish that? Apparently she had made up her mind. But Leah was ambitious, he thought, as a calculating look came into his eyes. There were things he could do for her.

A bribe? he thought, frowning. Although the idea left a bad taste in his mouth, Paul knew himself now. He would swallow the bad taste along with his pride and do anything he had to to keep her here.

Moments later he swung off the freeway onto the airport exit and felt the tension in his body grow. He would get there in time, he told himself. He had to. And when he found her, he would change her mind, even if he had to throw her over his shoulder and carry her off the plane.

Leah looked up when a man in a vinyl windbreaker sat down beside her. He bent over, wheezing as he tried to fit a large canvas bag under the seat in front of him; then he leaned back and shoved at it with his feet.

Won't he ever stop fidgeting? she wondered, clenching her teeth in annoyance.

Finally the bag was positioned to his satisfaction. Leaning back in the seat, he glanced at Leah and smiled. She immediately turned back to the window. He looked like a talker. If she was forced to talk, she would be rude, and the poor man didn't deserve that.

After a while a tall man in his early twenties took the aisle seat, and the two men struck up a conversation. Leah tried to tune them out, but bits and pieces kept getting through to her.

"Yeah, they're filming it in San Francisco. I was real lucky to get the part—not that it's all that big. But it could—"

"—was on television once. That's not the same as a movie, but it sure made me a celebrity in Jacksboro. My next-door neighbors—"

Leah closed her eyes, and instantly Paul's image rose before her. Dear God, she didn't want to go. *Paul, I love you so much. Why couldn't you have loved me just a little?*

"—the main character. That's the twist, you see. And wouldn't I have given my eyeteeth to play Merlin!"

Leah's hands clenched on the armrests. How much longer before the plane took off? Once they were in the air it would be easier.

"—modern language, modern dress. The Knights of the Round Table are a street gang who go around saving women and old people from rival gangs. Merlin lives in the park and gives advice to all the—"

What was Paul doing now? Leah wondered. How would he react this evening, when Charlotte gave him her letter? Her decision would matter to him, she assured herself. But would he feel any loss at all?

When she opened her eyes again, her vision blurred. Suddenly she felt the people and the airplane receding, sight and sound fading in and out around her.

* * *

Leah blinked, then blinked again. She was standing in a small clearing surrounded by trees. Directly in front of her an old man was bent over a small, black caldron that rested on the glowing coals of a camp fire.

He was dressed in green tights and a thigh-length, purple-and-gray tunic. His long thin beard was steel gray, a shade darker than the incredible hair that hung in waves past his shoulders. Several pencil-thin braids swung around his face as he moved.

In the distance Leah could still hear the buzz of voices from the plane, which left her with a slightly sick feeling of disorientation.

At that moment the old man looked up, his milky-blue eyes widening in surprise. "What are you doing here?"

"I don't know," she admitted hesitantly. "Where am I?"

"Camelot Park...a unique new camping experience. We have facilities for tents and recreational vehicles of all sizes. Also a twelve-acre lake—ignore the broad floating around in the water. She's just trying to get attention."

"And you are...?"

He stirred whatever was in the pot. "Some people call me the Wizard of the Woods, some call me The One Who Sees and Knows All, some just call me that weird old man." He glanced up. "You can call me Merlin."

"A dream," she said in resignation as her fears were confirmed. Then she frowned. "But it can't be. There wasn't a movie, and I don't think I'm even asleep. I can still hear the people on the plane talking."

He rolled his eyes. "Why do I get all the nuts?" He sighed. "I suppose you have a problem you want me to solve for you."

"I have problems," she said. "But I'd have to be pretty desperate to come to someone who looks like a cross between Rasputin and a punk rocker."

"And you're not that desperate?"

She closed her eyes, shivering suddenly. "Yes," she whispered. "Yes, I'm that desperate." Opening her eyes again, she met his gaze. "You see, I'm in love with—"

He waved a thin hand, cutting her off. "You don't have to tell me. I know all about you and Paul. What do you want me to do about it? I suppose I could turn him into an owl. It's a little hard to get worked up over a dumb bird."

"That's the best you have to offer?" she asked in disbelief. "I should have expected it. Your track record on relationships is not exactly wonderful. Arthur and Guinevere. Guinevere and Lancelot. Lancelot and Arthur, for that matter. Arthur and Guinevere died unhappy, and Lancelot became a nun or something."

"A monk, but it's an understandable mistake." His smooth pink brow wrinkled thoughtfully. "I always wondered about that boy. There was a rumor that he and Guinevere spent a lot of time playing checkers. And he was so *sensitive*. One word from the queen and he runs off naked and spends a couple of years in the woods eating acorns. Of course, he did manage to produce Galahad. But he was under a spell when that happened, and you can never tell what those idiot witches put in their potions. I knew one—''

When it looked as if he was going to slide into another anecdote from the past, Leah cleared her throat, drawing his attention back to her.

''The point is,'' he said sternly, ''when it comes to love, I can only give advice. Is it my fault that some people are too stubborn to listen to me?''

She bit her lip. She felt ridiculous talking to a figment of her imagination, but there had been truth in the other dreams. Couldn't she find truth in this one as well? It was possible that there was something buried in her own subconscious that could only come out in a dream.

''I'll listen,'' she said softly. ''Can you look into the future? Can you see if Paul will ever open up to me? If I go back and marry him, will he ever come to love me as much as I love him?''

His lips twisted in a strange smile, as though he knew something she didn't and pitied her for her ignorance. ''Then what you really want is to diminish his love?''

She studied him, considering his words. ''If you're trying to say he loves me, you're crazy.'' She paused. ''And even if he did, he couldn't possibly love me as much as I love him. I would die for him.''

"Maybe," he conceded. "But dying's easy. It's over in a few seconds. It's living for someone that's tough. He's willing to do that for you. But you? You're running away. I can only assume that means you don't love him enough."

She shook her head restlessly. He was confusing her. He was twisting the truth and making her sound like a paranoid fool.

"If I thought he really loved me," she whispered tightly, "I would never leave him. But he's closed himself off to human emotions. Why should I let myself be hurt over and over again by a man who only opens up to me in dreams?"

"You want a dream man? I take it you're not a Bette Midler fan."

"What does she have to do with anything?"

"*The Rose*. You know, the stuff about the dream that's afraid of waking up.... Oh, never mind," he said in exasperation. "So you love him, but you're a coward. I don't have time to waste on cowards. You can leave now."

She felt a wave of panic wash over her. She was positive she was close to something, to some kind of revelation. She couldn't wake up without finding out.

"No, wait...please. It's not really like that. You see, Paul holds part of himself back. It's his way. I can't expect him to change his character for me. How many times has Dear Abby said, 'Don't go into a marriage expecting your partner to change?' If they don't make the effort when love is fresh and exciting, why would they bother when it settles down to day-to-day routine? That makes sense. Doesn't it?''

Leah heard the pleading note in her voice. She wanted desperately for him to convince her that she was wrong about the future. She ached to go back to Paul.

"If Dear Abby said it, then it's right," he said firmly. "I trust her implicitly. In fact, I've sent her a few problems that had me stumped, and she always came through for me. But your situation doesn't fit that piece of advice. Paul doesn't need to change. He needs to trust you enough to bring that hidden part of himself out in the open. Have you ever shown him that he can trust you? No, of course you haven't. You've been holding back a part of yourself—your love—and then you whine because he does the same thing.''

Leah felt numb with shock. What Merlin said made sense. Paul wasn't as open as he had been in the dreams, but neither was she. She had been so busy thinking of herself, of her insecurities, that she hadn't given a thought to his. Had he sensed that she was holding back and been afraid, just as she had been afraid?

"If only I knew," she murmured, brushing a hand across her face. "I would give anything to know that what you're saying is the truth.''

"Okay, give me your firstborn child and I'll show you." When she glanced at him in confusion, he shrugged. "Just trying to lighten things up.''

He moved across the open ground and stopped beside her, his eyes gentle as he picked up her hand.

"You hurt so much," he said sadly. "And it's all so unnecessary." Shaking his head, making the little braids swirl, he smiled. "So you want a sign. That's what's wrong with people today. In my day, a magician's word was good enough. Now you all have to have proof."

He guided her toward the small caldron. "Come and look, Leah. Look inside the caldron and you'll have your sign."

She slowly lowered her eyes and looked at the bubbling liquid. "It's—" She frowned. "It's chicken-noodle soup."

"My lunch," he explained. "Just keep looking."

At that moment the pale liquid swirled violently, then settled into a surface as smooth and clear as glass. And there was Paul.

She caught her breath, bending closer. He was in the airport, moving quickly through the people. The tension in his face tore at her. She saw a muscle flicker beside his mouth, and suddenly she could hear his thoughts.

Don't let it be too late. I have to see her. I have to make her understand that this is right. Leah! You can't leave me now. You can't.

Leah felt the blood drain from her face, and she began to tremble. She raised her gaze to the old man beside her. "Is this the truth?" she asked hoarsely. "Is he really in the airport?"

He shrugged. "This is your dream. It's all coming out of your head and your heart. So you tell me, is it the truth?"

She passed a hand across her face in confusion. Then suddenly she knew. "It's the truth," she whispered. "He needs me. He *loves* me. I've got to get to him, Merlin. I've got to wake up now and get off the plane."

He frowned. "We may have a problem. The plane's already under way."

She swayed, then pulled herself up straight. "It can't be. I'll make them turn back. It won't be the same if I catch the next plane back. He would have to hurt too long. I can't let him go through that kind of pain." She clutched the magician's thin hand tightly. "Look, I know you're just a product of my subconscious. But Paul said we don't understand half of what the mind is capable of, so I'm asking you, if there's anything—*anything*—you can do, please help me."

He stared at her, his eyes worried. "I don't know. I'll try, Leah. But don't count on it."

"But I am counting on it," she said, her voice quiet and intense. "I've got to get back to him. I've got to."

* * *

"I'm sorry, the flight to San Francisco is taking off now. Is there anything else I can help you with?"

Paul turned away from the counter, the muscles of his face slack. He looked older. He felt older. Moving slowly, he walked to the line of chairs that were bolted to the floor and sat down, staring through the glass wall at the runway.

People moved past him and around him. He knew they were there, but somehow he couldn't feel their reality. As he sat, he let the pain sink in, then began to analyze it, poking it, testing it. He needed the pain. It was the only proof he had that he still existed. A wavering grayness shadowed the world. He blinked carefully, trying to make it go away, but it hung on stubbornly.

He had told Leah that he didn't believe in fate, but maybe fate had had a hand in his affairs after all. They had just missed connecting nine years ago. Now they had just missed connecting again.

He gave a short, harsh laugh. This was the kind of thing the old Greek gods enjoyed. They would throw in a hurricane or a two-headed monster just to see what the poor mortal who was their victim would so. Or they would give him a glimpse of heaven, then snatch it away to see if he would fall apart.

A man and woman in Universal uniforms stood behind him, talking. After a moment Paul focused on their conversation in an attempt to bring himself out of whatever dimension he had slipped into.

"—every instrument on the plane. Joe said it was the weirdest thing he's ever seen. They were taxiing down the runway, getting into position for the take-off, when the instruments just went haywire."

"But that doesn't make sense. They were checked less than two hours ago."

"Well, you can bet they're going to get checked again."

Paul leaned back. It hadn't worked. He had heard the words, but they meant nothing.

Suddenly he sat up straighter, frowning. He couldn't believe what he was doing. He was actually sitting there, accepting that it was over between him and Leah, accepting that this was his only chance with her. All his life he had fought for what he wanted. Now, when it concerned the most important thing in the world, he was going to calmly give up?

Not on your life, he told himself with iron determination. In relief, he felt the blood begin flowing in his veins again. He wouldn't give up. Not now, not ever. He would fight fate and destiny and any army that tried to keep him away from Leah.

But right now he would book a seat on the next flight out, he decided. He rose to his feet and moved toward the desk. Then something caught his eye, and he stopped in his tracks.

Leah was there, not ten feet away from him. His head jerked up, his heart pounding so hard his whole body shook.

As he watched, she turned in his direction. And when she saw him, her face began to glow with a joy so extravagant that it took his breath away. With an abrupt movement she dropped her bag and ran toward him.

Paul took two awkward steps forward and caught her in his arms, clasping her tightly against him. He felt her heart beating wildly, keeping perfect time with his as she shared his triumph. Now he knew that he wouldn't have to fight. Leah was his forever.

Epilogue

Reason becomes the marshal to my will,
And leads me to your eyes, where I o'erlook
Love's stories, written in love's richest book.

A Midsummer Night's Dream—Act II, Scene 3

P aul almost overlooked the small news item. It was only a couple of inches long, and placed in the bottom corner of the page, and it just happened to catch his eye as he turned the pages of the newspaper to get to the area business report. When he read it, he laughed aloud.

"What's so funny?"

He lowered the paper and looked across the breakfast table at his wife. Lately she had taken to wearing her hair pulled to the back of her head in a tight knot. She thought it gave her a more professional, more businesslike appearance. Paul didn't want to disillusion her, so he didn't tell her that the pale fluff resting on the nape of her neck was so sensual that every man who saw her was tempted to kiss it.

His wife, he thought, smiling. Paul would never get tired of the words. They had been married for almost six months, and he kept waiting for his feelings for her to become a warm, comfortable habit, to become ordinary, but it hadn't happened. Every time he looked at her, he felt happiness explode inside him.

"I love you, Leah," he said, his voice husky.

He could see the reaction in her face: an instant, melting softness. Then, sitting up straighter, she assumed a haughty expression, arching one eyebrow in inquiry. "And you find that funny?"

"No, I find that wonderful, but perfectly natural. How could I not love you?" he asked. "It was a news report that made me laugh. Come and look."

"You could read it to me," she suggested. "Then I wouldn't have to make the long trip around the table. Or you could simply hand me the paper."

"Those are both viable alternatives," he agreed, his face solemn. "But if you come over here to read it, you get to sit in my lap, and I get to do exciting things to your body while you read."

She wiped her mouth with her napkin, then laid it down and stood up. "I see your point."

A few moments later he murmured against her lips, "Aren't you going to read the article?"

Leah outlined his mouth with tip of her tongue. "Is what's in it better than kissing you?"

He chuckled. "No, but it's the official results of the investigation into the instrument malfunction on the Universal flight to San Francisco."

She held his face between her hands, smoothing her thumbs across his cheekbones. Leah loved his face. She never got tired of looking at him. There was so much strength in this face, she thought. It was in his eyes that the vulnerability showed. Green eyes that would burn with passion or glow with a love deeper than any she had ever imagined possible.

Meeting those green eyes, she said, "I love official results. What did they decide?"

"A freak magnetic disturbance."

"That sounds nice and official," she said, nodding slowly. "What do you think?"

He smiled. "Merlin's magic, or magnetism." He shook his head slightly. "I don't understand either one. But I don't care what caused it. The results are what count."

He was right, Leah thought. None of it mattered. The dreams that had caused so much confusion were now only a distant memory. She couldn't even recall them clearly. Loving Paul and having him love her back were reality. It didn't matter how they had found each other; all that mattered was that they had.

"Leah?"

"Yes?" The word was a breathless whisper.

His arms tightened around her. "That sound like a bedroom yes."

"Was it a bedroom question?"

"No, it was a boardroom question."

"Sounds dull," she said, then pulled back a little to study his face. "What's bothering you?"

He removed her hand from his neck and brought it to his lips. "The San Francisco job," he said. "It makes me uncomfortable knowing that you gave it up for me. It makes me feel selfish."

"It makes you feel selfish because you *are* selfish—where I'm concerned," she added when she felt him stiffen. "Just as I'm selfish where you're concerned. I think we need to take a trip to visit some rocks and dirt. Remember how it feels out there? Promotions, raises and status—those are not the main part of our lives." She met his eyes earnestly. "The main part of our life is us. Us—together. The rest are frills... perks... inconsequential additions."

He buried his face in her throat. "Yes," he said roughly. "That's it exactly."

"Besides," she said, her eyes sparkling, "I have my eye on another position at Universal."

He frowned. The Frown. But now it only made her laugh. "What position?"

"Vice president of marketing," she said, her voice carefully casual.

For a moment he looked startled, almost wary. Then suddenly he stood up with her in his arms and laughed all the way to the bedroom.

* * * * *

COMING NEXT MONTH

Silhouette Classics

**The best books from the past by
your favorite authors.**

The first two stories of a delightful collection...

#1 DREAMS OF EVENING by Kristin James

As a teenager, Erica had given Tonio Cruz all her love, body and soul, but he betrayed and left her anyway. Ten years later, he was back in her life, and she quickly discovered that she still wanted him. But the situation had changed—now she had a son. A son who was very much like his father, Tonio, the man she didn't know whether to hate—or love.

#2 INTIMATE STRANGERS by Brooke Hastings

Rachel Grant had worked hard to put the past behind her, but Jason Wilder's novel about her shattered her veneer of confidence. When they met, he turned her life upside down again. Rachel was shocked to discover that Jason wasn't the unfeeling man she had imagined. Haunted by the past, she was afraid to trust him, but he was determined to write a new story about her—one that had to do with passion and tenderness and love.

Take 4 Silhouette Desire novels
and a surprise gift
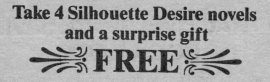

Then preview 6 brand-new Silhouette Desire novels—delivered to your door as soon as they come off the presses! If you decide to keep them, you pay just $2.24 each*—a 10% saving off the retail price, *with no additional charges for postage and handling!*

Silhouette Desire novels are not for everyone. They are written especially for the woman who wants a more satisfying, more deeply involving reading experience. Silhouette Desire novels take you beyond the others.

Start with 4 Silhouette Desire novels and a surprise gift absolutely FREE. They're yours to keep without obligation. You can always return a shipment and cancel at any time.

Simply fill out and return the coupon today!

* Plus 69¢ postage and handling per shipment in Canada.

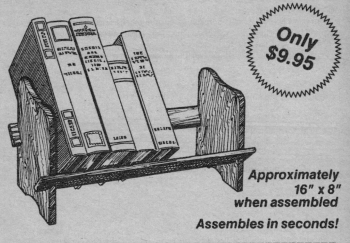

Silhouette Special Edition

COMING NEXT MONTH

#421 NO ROOM FOR DOUBT—Tracy Sinclair
No job too small or too difficult, Stacey Marlowe's ad boasted. But then she hadn't considered the demands her first customer would make. Shady Sean Garrison wanted—of all things!—her trust.

#422 INTREPID HEART—Anne Lacey
Trent Davidson would forever be a hero to Vanessa Hamilton. After all, he'd twice saved her life. But how could Trent settle for Vanessa's childlike adoration when he needed her womanly love?

#423 HIGH BID—Carole Halston
Katie Gamble was thrilled when fellow building contractor Louis McIntyre reentered her life. But Louis's gentle deception—and uneasy memories of a night long ago—threatened their bid for a future together.

#424 LOVE LYRICS—Mary Curtis
Ambitious lyricist Ashley Grainger lived and breathed Broadway, while her former fiancé, conservative lawyer Zachary Jordan, was Boston born and bred. Despite their renewed duet of passion, could they possibly find a lasting harmony?

#425 SAFE HARBOR—Sherryl Woods
When sexy neighbor Drew Landry filed a complaint about Tina Harrington's unorthodox household, they battled it out in the boardroom . . . and the bedroom . . . even as they longed for sweet compromise.

#426 LAST CHANCE CAFE—Curtiss Ann Matlock
Rancher Wade Wolcott wanted no part of Ellie McGrew's struggle to build a new life for her daughters. But the lovely, unassuming widow bought the farm next door, waited tables in his diner—and somehow crept into his heart.

AVAILABLE THIS MONTH: